Survival

Also by this author:

Kings Cross (2015) Book Guild
The Shropshire Stalker (2016) You Caxton
I Am Lucy (2018) You Caxton

Survival

Nick Jones

This is a work of fiction. Names and characters are the product of the author's imagination and any resemblance to actual persons, living or dead, is entirely coincidental.

ISBN: 978-1-917293-89-1

Cover design by
Tee Blake
kreativiteedesign@gmail.com

CONTENTS

PREFACE

AS WELL AS the countless acts of kindness from friends who have visited or lived in Australia, I must place on record the inspiration I got from three books associated with that continent.

Michael Thornton's *Jackeroo* (Penguin Books) is an excellent introduction to the gruelling outdoor life of a hired ranch-hand in Central Victoria, tending huge herds of merino sheep. It is almost worth tracking it down for the chapter on shearing.

A much earlier work (published in 1937) is William Hatfield's beautifully crafted *I Find Australia* (Oxford University Press), an absorbing account of an Englishman's experiences in the saddle as a cattle chargehand on the Western Plains.

Last, but by no means least, is David Hill's *The Forgotten Children* (Allen & Unwin), a harrowing first-hand account of the shameful Assisted Passages Migration scheme for WWII orphans, created by the UK-based Fairbridge Society, which operated the draconian Farm School system.

Rob McAuley's illustrated nautical history of sea travel *The Liners* (Boxtree) was an invaluable reference source. Special thanks are also due to Coventry City's Archives.

There are many contenders in the twentieth century for ill-advised examples of what is sometimes euphemistically termed 'social engineering'.

The Chinese government's suppression of Falun Gong; General Augustus Pinochet's method of removing Chile's dissident trade union leaders (fly them out over the Pacific Ocean and push them out of the plane without a parachute); the chilling experiments on embryos by Auschwitz's head clinician Josef Mengale; or the post-war British government's crackpot notion that Caribbean islanders could make up our shortage of bus conductors if transported to Britain on the *Empire Windrush*.

But the joint Australian-British initiative to transport UK war orphans – some as young as 7 years old – to Australia for £10 'to start a new life', must surely be in the running for an Oscar.

The scheme was eventually dismantled as a result of joint action by the Australian and British governments, but it took us 25 years to own up to the mistake, when Prime Minister Gordon Brown told survivors: "We let you down." **NJ**

1

ALAN

CHARTERED SURVEYOR Alan Jones – Alan Henry Evan Jones to give him his full title – was Edwardian to the core. Edwardian bearing and manners, a stickler for etiquette and dying-out conventions - like opening doors for ladies or standing when they entered the room. He was a stern disciplinarian, with corporal punishment still very much on his domestic agenda.

Alan was a natty dresser. He had a wardrobe full of Savile Row suits, shirts from Burlington Arcade, gold cuff links from Aspreys and hand-made shoes from Jermyn Street. His preference for silk socks, supported by calf-length suspenders, was one penchant which always mystified his wife Mimi.

At the outbreak of the second World War – before many of his friends were called up – Alan was seconded to the government's War Damage Commission, spending his office-bound time assessing claims by building owners. By night, he was air-spotting as an ARP volunteer, with his night-time vigils (watching for incoming German bombers) spent atop the turret of Wanstead's Parish church of St Mary's, a short cycle ride from his mother's rambling Edwardian house which overlooked The Green, Wanstead.

Alan's son Nicholas had seen for some time how the work at the War Damage Commission had been getting his father down. The long hours at the Commission's offices in Finsbury Square and the heartbreaking daily grind of site inspections to buildings flattened by the Blitz. On his desk at home at Eagle Court he had a small framed photo of a newspaper image which had gone around the world. It showed King George VI in naval uniform, standing on top of an enormous pile of bricks, with Queen Elizabeth, in a cream two-piece and a white woollen top coat, matching hat and even a string of pearls, standing at his side.

They could easily have been parachuted in from Royal Ascot. According to Alan a large bank in the City had taken a direct hit during one of the Luftwaffe's night raids. The King and Queen were up early and insisted on being taken to the scene. When he was in a reflective mood he would sometimes say to his son: "If they can make the effort to be on duty by 9.00 am then I should too."

International sportsmen and sportswomen – as Nicholas learned to his cost – were conversational topics best avoided at the family's Sunday lunch table. Henry Cotton, his father avowed, was a better golfer than Ben Hogan. He wasn't. Jack Hobbs was a better batsman than Donald Bradman. He wasn't. And Fred Perry was a better singles player than Lew Hoad. Which he wasn't.

Partly out of sheer bravado Nick had formed the eccentric idea that, after Churchill, what post-war Britain needed was a charismatic leader like Fidel Castro to make it great again. He kept a perfectly straight face after making this observation one Sunday lunchtime, causing the Head of the Household to have a violent coughing fit, before being advised by his wife to go and lie down for half-an-hour. Mimi's sister Denise's Labour-supporting husband Tommy thought Herbert Morrison would make an excellent PM ("But he was a co-founder of the 'No Conscription' campaign," Alan once spluttered over a frigid family lunch).

Whilst punishments at Nick's local boarding school (Forest School) were both routine and nonsensical (eg: learning 21 lines by rote from a text book for failing to have the middle button of your school jacket done up), 'home punishments' dispensed by Alan Jones came in all shapes and sizes and were not always proportionate with the offence. The cane was routinely used and Nick's father (who had been a boxing 'blue' at his school) employed a mean right cross which used to come from nowhere, invariably knocking his son off his feet. Visits to the cinema or London jazz haunts were regularly ruled out if the boy was thought to have contributed little towards domestic chores. Alan Jones (himself no mean exponent of the *'mot just'* in grown-up company), would never tolerate amusing quips made by his son. These were usually dismissed as 'Smart Alec remarks'.

One of the most spiteful punishments meted out by the Master of the House was when Nick was banned from taking up the offer of a night petrol pump attendant at a local garage, on these laughable grounds: "How do you suppose it would look if one of my friends pulled in for petrol one evening and saw my son on the pumps?"

2

MIMI

ALAN AND MIMI had been married for three years when Nicholas came along. Theirs had not been a whirlwind romance, though by plodding Alan's standards it was certainly speedy.

After successfully avoiding being rounded up by the Germans in their home town of Liege, Mimi and her parents crossed the Channel to Dover on a night ferry and then, as homeless asylum seekers, were billeted in New Cross in south London. Mimi's father Joseph (a skilled cabinetmaker) had no trouble landing a job as a Foreman in a furniture factory, while his wife Jean took in lodgers. But 18-year-old Mimi had no discernible career path (her education at a convent had been perfunctory) and Joseph was determined not to have her conscripted into a women's army unit. Dunkirk had already demonstrated that this war was certainly going to last as long as the previous conflict.

On a day off from domestic chores her mother took Mimi to London's West End for the first time. Apart from the barrage balloons hovering over Hyde Park and the near-total absence of private motor cars, there were few signs in Mayfair that there was a war on. They walked north up Bond Street. Opposite Sotheby's boarded-up auction rooms was a men's hairdressers, tucked away in a basement. At the head of the stairs a neatly-lettered card announced: "Maurice, Gentlemen's Hairdresser, urgently requires an apprentice manicurist. Pay and conditions by negotiation."

The two women looked at each other. Mimi first wondered if her mother might be tiring of the board-and-lodging trade. It was arduous hours but it paid the bills. Then the penny dropped. "Me?" she squealed. "I couldn't possibly!" But her mother wasn't taking 'no' for an answer and led her firmly by the hand down into Maurice's basement salon - a brightly-lit space smelling strongly of men's hair oil and cologne. Framed signed portrait photos of celebrities lined the walls: by the looks of the collection Maurice had a star-spangled clientele. There was Larry Adler, jazz pianist Leslie 'Hutch' Hutchinson and in gleaming cricket whites Surrey and England's Bedser twins, Alec and Eric. Mozambique crooner Al Bowlly – killed in an air raid – would become Mimi's favourite client.

In her heavy accent Mother Jean did the negotiating very skilfully. Any payment of indentures was out of the question she told the elderly proprietor. He stroked his chin and looked at smartly turned-out Mimi, considering his final offer.

"Well, Madame Pacquay, if Mimi would be prepared to report here for work at 9 sharp every weekday morning – we're closed on Saturdays – I will give her a start without salary on a six-month trial," adding the incentive: "and she can keep all her tips." The incentive did the trick and the deal was sealed with smiles and handshakes all round. "Let's go to Selfridges' Copper Kettle cafeteria to celebrate, shall we?" said the jubilant mother to her daughter.

3

ARMAGEDON IN E11

AT THE END of his night-watching shift on the roof of St Mary's, Alan Jones rang his wife from his mother's house in Wanstead. "I'm just grabbing a tea at Mother's then I'll be on my way."

"Well, I'm afraid there's been a slight change of plan. Woodford ARP rang. They want you at a new strike."

"Where?"

"Churchill Gardens at the bottom of Eagle Lane. Direct hit. A VII."

"'Oh dear. Did they say anything about injuries or fatalities?"

"No. Just for you to get there as soon as possible."

"Right. I'll be there by midnight. Tell Nick to bring me a flask of coffee in the morning."

"I certainly will. And some freshly baked scones?"

"Rather!" That was the last word Mimi would ever hear from her husband.

He could hardly have missed the site of the VII strike on the apartment block on the corner of Eagle Lane, a stone's throw from the old Eagle Hotel coaching inn. The whole corner was lit up like a Hollywood film set, with tall arc lights illuminating the debris and rubble and rescue workers moving through it like worker ants. Very little of the four-storey building had survived the impact.

All the emergency services were there: the fire brigade with two escape ladders; ambulances from Whipps Cross Hospital; ARP personnel and a gaggle of black Wolseley police cars. Alan propped his cycle against some brick rubble and slipped on his white helmet. His old friend Harold Bostock wandered over, looking utterly exhausted. "Morning Alan. Well, talk about 'the luck of the Gods'. Virtually all the residents were in their basement air raid shelter, bar a disabled couple and a toddler which the parents had inexplicably left in its cot."

"So only three fatalities?"

"Yes, but that's still three too many."

The old man, looking none too steady on his feet, gingerly negotiated his way through the rubble as a police chief approached Alan Jones. "How long can you stay, Alan?"

"All night if necessary."

"Good man! There's a couple of sniffer dogs on their way over from Chingford. I want the rubble marked out with white tapes and we'll double check we haven't missed anyone." Alan gave him a semi-salute as he traipsed off.

Cycle-mad Nicholas was nearing the end of his last summer holiday from Forest School, where he boarded – much to all his schoolfriends' astonishment, given that his parent's home was less than two miles from the school gates. What Nick didn't own up to was that Forest's primitive dormitories and spartan meals were nothing in comparison to his father's stern Edwardian regime. Going to Saturday night jazz raves at the Cook's Ferry Inn on Walthamstow Marshes, for example, was a doddle by bike from Forest School – an 'illegal' break-out which would have been hard to pull off from Eagle Court.

In the holidays Nick spent a lot of time in his father's garage, working on and adding accessories to his racing bike – a stripped-down British-built Dayton Flyer. The Dayton (which, during the summer holidays, had magically changed colour from red and white to a metal-flake-finished emerald green) shared space with his father's treasured cream Rover 90 Tourer, which would be buffed with Simonize every Sunday afternoon after its weekly trip to Wanstead Golf Club. Every four years, bedecked with blue ribbons, it was the lead car in the pool of vehicles which were used to ferry Wanstead and Woodford's elderly and infirm to the polls, to re-elect their Member of Parliament, Winston Churchill.

The level crossing gates at the top of Eagle Lane were closed, with signals set for an approaching train. Nick was seated on a low garden wall in front of a bungalow, whose curtains were drawn closed. White window tape criss-crossed the glazing and there was no sign of life from within. It was just after 8.30 am and he decided to have a swig of the black coffee from the Thermos flask his mother had just handed him. As he was finishing, an oldish man in scruffy working clothes and with a morning stubble, pushing a worse-for-wear BSA bike, stood in front of him eyeing him suspiciously. The stranger took a half-smoked roll-up from behind his ear and lit it. "Don't I know you?"

"I don't think so."

"D'you play golf?"

"No. Cricket and cycling are my sports."

"I'm the Groundsman at Wanstead Golf Club. I could swear I've seen you down by The Basin - the lake at the 14th by Overton Drive." Nick idly spun one of the bike's pedals and tucked his jean bottoms into his white socks, signalling his intention to leave.

"Now 'ang about!" The stranger pointed menacingly. "I've got it. You don't by any chance own a pair of white frogman's flippers and a blue rubber underwater mask?"

Bang to rights. "Possibly."

"Then I've gotcha my lad! My mate Banks, who's chief bar steward at the golf club, says e's seen you of a Sunday morning dragging a big waterproof bag full of golf balls out that lake. 'e said you was wearing blue trunks and was carrying white flippers." He shook his head in admiration. "I'll tell you what - old Banksy don't miss a detail." He stubbed his cigarette out on the garden wall.

There didn't seem to be any point in side-stepping this old busybody. "What of it?"

"What OF IT'? Why that's thieving!"

"I'd call it recovering unclaimed lost property. Like finding an umbrella on a bus."

The old man gave a dismissive scoff at this last remark. "The wilful purloining of a person's property – whether it be an umbrella or a golf ball - requires the finder to take all reasonable steps to reunite the owner with his or her property." At one point he was actually clutching the frayed collar of his cardigan like a barrister. Nick decided he'd had enough of this tedious Speak-Your-Weight machine. The argumentative groundsman remained perched on the bungalow's dwarf front wall. Across the track cars were now backing up across the entrance to the local coal yard, waiting for the level crossing gates to open.

Just then the sky darkened and they heard the deep bass drone of an approaching machine. Much louder than a train. A long black tubular object passed from right to left above their heads parallel with the ground and barely at chimney top level. The engine noise suddenly cut out, but the object remained eerily on its horizontal trajectory, heading for the bottom of Eagle Lane and the bomb-damaged Churchill Gardens, still busy with rescue activity.

The 'flying tube' with its black quartered fuselage and white rear fins, cast a sinister shadow down the traffic-clogged side road. Moments later, like a choreographed ballet, all the trees in the suburban gardens swayed in unison, some shedding substantial branches. A pause of two or three seconds was followed by a devastating, ear-splitting explosion. Nick, who had been about to set off on his bike, was blown off his feet into the bungalow's front garden, while the grumpy groundsman finished up dazed and half-conscious in the goldfish pool. The tinkle of breaking window glass seemed to go on forever. And then a long dense column of black smoke snaked up from the direction of Churchill Gardens. With pin-point accuracy, Pas-de-Calais' second mission of destruction had been delivered to exactly the same location as the first, twelve hours earlier.

Nick lifted his bike out of the garden. As the road was liberally dusted with foliage and broken glass he opted to carry it on his shoulder and headed for the subway. Every dog in Eagle Lane was barking.

When he reached the back of the deserted Eagle Garage with its shattered car showroom window, he propped the green Dayton against an inside wall to complete the morbid journey of discovery on foot. One of his cycle shoes snagged on a metal object almost as big as a gold ball. He picked it up. It was still warm, dark brown and grooved like a lump of iron pyrites. He pocketed the fresh piece of shrapnel.

The rescue site's arc lamps had all been wrecked but in the early morning it was possible to discern the 'worker ants' now attending to fresh casualties. Stretcher bearers were carrying fatalities to the ambulances. Clearly the second VII attack, with pin-point accuracy onto the same target, had resulted in a greater loss of life.

There was precious little of Churchill Gardens left standing. As for its inspiration, he looked in a very sorry state: the solid bronze life-size image of the wartime leader leaned perilously forward over the pavement. If it hadn't been for the fact that the artist had clothed him in his 'signature' boiler suit, the Prime Minister could have been making a debating point in the House of Commons.

Eventually Nick located his father, sitting forlornly on a pile of rubble, being administered by a young Nigerian nurse. A Sister stood alongside checking his pulse. "Alan?" He barely recognised his name, like a prize fighter reluctant to go another round. "Nurse will dress that gash you've got on the back of the cranium, but then I really think we need to get you admitted to Whipps for a scan." Nick stepped up and clasped his father on the shoulder, a gesture which the older man responded to with a smile.

"Can he have some coffee, Sister?" Nick asked. She nodded. "Of course."

His father tucked into the scones with relish. "Well done, Nick. You made it then?"

"Yes Father."

He shook his head and wiped away the crumbs. "Sadly, old Harold Bostock didn't. They've just taken him away." It was starting to rain. Nick just wanted to leave the scene of this evil carnage.

After spending two days recuperating in bed at home in Eagle Court, Nick's father died in the night from an acute aneurysm. His funeral service 10 days later, at St Mary's Church, Wanstead, was a double funeral shared with his lifetime friend Harold Bostock, attended by over 200 mourners.

4

THE WAKE

THE GUESTS STARTED to arrive at Rozel shortly after 12 o'clock, having walked down St Mary's Avenue from the parish church. Roughly half the mourners were from Alan's side, with an equally large contingent from the Bostock family. On leaving St Mary's the entire congregation processed down the centre of St Mary's Avenue, led by a Highland piper, before the Bostock mourners peeled off and headed across The Green for the family house in Chestnut Avenue. A late arrival at Rozel was Alan's brother-in-law Bob Stewart, a tea grower from Colombo. He had made a lightening dash back to England by air with Imperial Airways.

Home help Alice had worked her elbow grease magic with Silvo on Rozel's huge silver collection (several were Alan's golfing trophies), all displayed on the Bechstein grand piano in the drawing room. Former home help Moira and Alice's daughter Poppy greeted the mourners in the hall with a glass of sherry before ushering them into the large dining room which overlooked Wanstead Green. A huge mahogany dining table (normally only used at Christmas) was piled high with savoury nibbles, sponge cakes and choux pastry chocolate eclairs (the latter most definitely out of Nana Belle's 600-page 'bible': *Mrs Beaton's Household Management*).

Unctuous family solicitor Vivian did all the introductions, while Grandma Belle, flanked by her sisters Ada and Annie, sat at the head of the table. It was just like Christmas, but not half so jolly. The sisters were on small glasses of a wine cup, while Nana Belle was already on her second gin and mixed vermouth. She beckoned Nick to her side. "I'll have a refill, dear. And while your outside just ring my bookmaker and find out what won the 12 o'clock at Uttoxeter, would you?"

Having discharged her door-opening duties Scots Moira had retreated to the back garden with Nick's best friend Matthew. The couple appeared to be deep in conversation by Grandma's vegetable patch. Having barely exchanged half-a-dozen sentences with this Scottish nymphet, Nick was irked that his best mate seemed to have snatched her from under his nose.

Alan's oldest friend Bill Worthy delivered the Encomium. Word-perfect and without notes. Mimi gripped Nick's arm and quietly piped an eye.

A surprise guest was Nick's headmaster at Forest School, Gerald Miller. He cornered Nick and asked him about his structural engineering aspirations. Nick was too non-plussed to confess that it was now 'domestic funding' considerations which had brought forward his plan to seek a place at Walthamstow Technical College.

"Leave it with me," the Head said reassuringly. "I think I can get it past the Governors. Might even be able to fix a small bursary to cover your last term's fees." In a social setting, dark-suited dapper Major Miller MC was a nice enough cove (no-one at Forest had ever discovered how the Military Cross had been won); but in his black gown, seated behind the desk in his study, with an array of canes lined up on the wall, he was a force to be reckoned with.

"I would appreciate that very much, sir," said Nick, excusing himself to fetch more food from the kitchen – and find out what won the 12 o'clock at Uttoxeter. Nick slipped a refill in front of his grandmother. "Marc Deveraux on Chantilly Lace."

"Never heard of him. What were the odds?"

"12-1."

She scoffed (though secretly envious of the odds). "Rank outsider."

Food stocks were running low (the chief sandwich-maker having taken leave of absence to discuss raising rhubarb with Nick's best friend) but the drinks department was holding up manfully. Shortly after 2.30 pm the coast was clear. Alice had started the washing up – with Poppy drying; Ada and Annie had both nodded off under the influence of Nick's lethally-strong wine cup; and Grandma Belle was furiously searching the pages of *Sporting Life* to find out who this Monsieur Deveraux was.

Matt, having belatedly recognised that he hadn't exactly pulled his weight during the proceedings, offered to guide the two tottering sisters to a waiting taxi and accompany them home to Forest Gate.

Nick slipped away from the kitchen mele to take refuge in the large workshop over Rozel's garage. Seated back on her usual 'throne' in the kitchen, with all the best china safely stowed away – but still affronted that an upstart called Deveraux should have had a 12-1 winner - the Mistress of the House handed Alice her usual cut glass cocktail goblet: "When he's finished seeing Ada and Annie off, get Nicholas to give me a top-up of my usual would you, dear?" Matt caught up with him in the workshop on his return from Forest Gate. "Here you are! So, this is your little hideaway is it?"

Nick was holding a paint brush, mid-way through re-painting a Dunlop 65 golf ball he had retrieved from the bed of the lake on Wanstead Golf Course.

"Sort of. None of the others ever come up here and Grandma certainly couldn't manage those wooden steps. Good, isn't it?"

"I'll say."

Formed beneath the exposed rafters of the garage roof, the walls of the spacious workshop were lined with well-worn oak work benches, above which hung a huge array of carpenters' tools set on racks. A large oriel window at the front looked out onto The Green. Alan's father Henry, a master builder from Swansea, had seen the potential of the south-facing building plot looking out onto open space. The chosen name of the spacious homestead he built in 1900 was the Channel Islands resort where he and Isabelle had honeymooned. Four equally spacious detached houses separated Rozel from the dual carriageway that led west, to Gants Hill and Ilford.

Marking the corner of The Green was a distinctive Art Deco-styled building, destined to become a new station for the London Underground, but whose construction had been curtailed by the outbreak of war. It was now shielded by high wire security fencing, with a single sign warning PLESSEYS. KEEP OUT.

On a free-standing bench in the centre of Rozel's workshop Nick had fashioned a square slab of elm, routing it out with a 'grid' of 25 semi-spherical recesses, each with a salvaged golf ball in it – half painted and half washed clean. Nick explained to Matt that Phase Two of his ingenious restoration process involved drying the re-painted balls on a frame he had made from Meccano and chicken wire. "And the neat thing is that the spacing of the chicken wire is just a bit smaller than the balls. All I'm missing is a pair of kitchen tongs to turn them over. Then when they're dry, I just clean out the painting mould with turps and a rag."

"As your Financial Adviser, I have to say I think you're letting them go far too cheaply," Matt observed. Though neither youth would admit it to the other, 'restoration' was a euphemism for 'stolen and repainted'.

Nick continued painting unhurriedly. "What do you suggest?"

"Ten-and-six; and only orders of half-a-dozen." Nick paused mid-brush stroke, pursed his lips and squinted to consider Matt's suggestion.

"Six balls for half a guinea, delivered to your door by post - and probably only used once. It's not to be sneezed at. Cuts out the middle man." This was a reference to the Golf Club's Assistant Professional, who was privy to the scheme and who had been quietly purchasing Nick's reconditioned balls for use in the club's driving practice shed.

Nick continued spotting with the white paint. "Trouble is, there been a slight…. 'development'."

"Oh yes. What's that?"

"I was spotted last Sunday by the Club's Head Barman on his way to work at the clubhouse. And he's 'grassed' me to the Groundsman. Miserable old git. We were sitting on a wall in Eagle Lane, with him reading me the riot act about how I was stealing when that VII came over."

"What happened?"

Nick chuckled at the memory. "I left him unconscious in a goldfish pool. Listen, let's leave them at 1/6d each for the time being, shall we? Let the dust settle, so to speak." He put down his brush. "Any news on the Rover?"

"Yup. My brother-in-law says it's all set up with a rich old geezer out at Epping who's starting a veteran and vintage collection. British marques only. He can't wait to come and pick it up."

"Are you happy with the price?"

"Sure. Kevin says we might get a little more if he punted it around to all the second-hand dealers. But sooner or later the word's going to get out when someone recognises it as Alan's motor."

Nick began painting again. "Yeah, it's distinctive, isn't it? The ivory bodywork finish certainly appealed to his love of ostentation. Fine. £650 it is. We'll have to do the handover when Mother's next away for the day. She's talking about meeting up in London with her sister Denise."

"Fine. Now tell me - have you found the log book yet?"

Nick stopped painting again. "Err no. Still searching. It's bound to be in the flat somewhere. Either in his office – which I dread starting on as its just mountains of old WDC files – or in his chest of drawers in the bedroom. I might look there first." He dropped his paint brush in a jar of turps. "Any news about his set of golf clubs which I manage to smuggle out of Wanstead Golf Club?"

"Yup. My neighbour the lovely Lucinda wants to buy them as a surprise birthday present for her Hubbie. She's offered £180, which is precisely half what Lillywhites in Piccadilly told her a new Henry Cotton set – 8 irons, three woods and a putter – costs now. What d'you think?"

"Will she budge?"

"I very much doubt it."

"OK. Sold to the lady from Chigwell! He turned and smiled at Matthew. "Any other business?"

"No, that's about it. Do you realise, mate, that if we pull off these two sales we'll have almost £1000 – tax free - in the kitty? So just make sure you locate that log book."

Two hours later Nick rang Matthew at his parent's house just as he walked in. "Make that £1000 £1500 now. I found the log book tucked away behind some of his silk socks. And guess what?"

"What?"

"Inside every pair of socks there was a roll of 5 crisp white fivers. Ten sock rolls in all."

"S'truth – your Old Man was a hoarder and no mistake."

"King Magpie!"

“I’ll drop round with Lucinda’s dosh in the morning.”

“Make it after 9.00 would you, mate; I’m well behind with my cycle training schedule.”

5

THE GEORGE

IF THE MYSTERIOUS Plessey plant was one of Wanstead's unsolved wartime mysteries, the mighty George public house, which made the opposite corner at this busy junction leading down to Ilford, was an open book: a showy high-Victorian road house, probably inspired by Liverpool's iconic Philharmonic, designed by Walter Aubrey Thomas and completed in 1900. It had the same white tiled mosaic floors, moulded mahogany counters and brass foot rails and gold-braided crimson drapes hanging at the side of all the long acid-etched windows. Comfortable crimson velvet banquettes provided the seating. The polished copper plumbing in the men's toilets, set on jade green terrazzo wall panels, was a work of art.

Left over from the national VE celebrations, the Lounge Bar's shelves were still edged in red, white and blue tinsel. Pride of place on one of the shelves were signed photos of Max Miller and George Robey. Externally, the gin palace's slate-clad dome made it one of this East London's suburb's most striking buildings.

Cheek-by-jowl with The George was the diminutive Kinema – briefly an unsuccessful roller-skating rink and now struggling as an independent 'art house' cinema, specialising in X-rated foreign films and American Westerns. Until her infirmity, Grandma Jones had been a regular mid-week customer, usually nodding off during the dialogue, to be awoken by the gun fight in the finale.

Mine host at The George was Raj, an avuncular Indian. The pub's core clientele were the Plessey workers, led by their Chargehand Doreen, who would march them in like a drill sergeant at 5.00 pm as Raj was unlocking the frosted glass double doors. "First shout's on me tonight girls; you all did well - 144 again," she'd announce cheerily.

Nick, who had been hoping for a quiet pint before going to the cinema next door with Matt and Moira, had settled into a corner banquette, intent on catching up on a preview feature of the forthcoming Tour de France. A shadow fell across his cycling magazine. "All on your own, handsome?" asked a buxom young woman wearing a pale blue turban and a white coat marked 'Chargehand'.

"Oi, leave 'im alone Dor, you baby-snatcher," came a call from the bar, followed by much ribald cackling from the Chargehand's troupe.

Nick looked up and smiled. "I'm waiting for some friends. We're going next door to The Kinema."

"What's on?"

"*The Outlaw*."

"Good movie. Jane Russell," said the chargehand knowingly. "I'd join you if I didn't have to get this lot back to Gants Hill."

In the absence of Matthew and Moira, and realising that all chances of reading his cycling feature in peace were gone, Nick decided he'd better be sociable by offering the lady a drink. "A shandy would be nice," she purred in a strong Essex twang, settling herself down on the crimson velvet banquette beside him. "I'm Doreen, by the way."

"Pleased to meet you. I'm Nick." He wasn't in the mood to elaborate and soon returned with her drink.

"And where do you live, Nick?"

"Snaresbrook. You?"

"Gants Hill. I've got a small flat behind the Odeon. And are you at college?"

"Forest School. My final year. Then I want to study to be a structural engineer." He didn't feel like telling her about his dream of designing the North Sea's first oil rig.

He finished his shandy and just wished Matt and Moira would come and rescue him. "I hope you don't mind me asking, but what exactly do you and your colleagues make in that factory over the road?"

She gave a smirk as if she'd been asked this question a hundred times. "Christmas decorations."

"Really? Who for?"

"All sorts."

"Gamages and Hamleys?"

"Hell no. We're a world exporter – aren't we girls?" she called out to the gaggle at the bar.

"You bet!" came the chorus.

"Where does all this go on?"

"Mostly in the tunnels, though they built us a washroom and locker area in what was to have been the central concourse at the bottom of the escalators. And we've got air conditioning."

Nick nodded towards the bar. "And are they all Essex girls?"

"Nearly all of 'em. Dark-skinned Rita's from Columbia; and Gina's from Poland."

"And how do you move the stuff about. Fork lifts?"

Doreen shook her head. "Far too risky. If a steel lifting fork made a spark on the floor, the lot would go up. It would be like Guy Fawkes night on Wanstead Green. No, we've got our own battery-powered narrow-gauge railway. Gina's the driver." Doreen lifted her glass to toast Gina. "Poop poop!" As if to show her seniority (as a sergeant major might do with his stripes), she 'plumped up' the shoulder pads beneath her Plessey coat. "For my sins I have to look after that lot." Relief was at hand as at that moment Matt and Moira walked into the bar of The George.

"Ready for *The Outlaw?*" Moira asked.

"I certainly am." Standing up Nick briefly introduced the couple to Doreen.

"Nice meeting you," he assured the Chargehand none too convincingly.

"Hope we bump into each other again", Doreen purred, making it sound more like a wish than a pleasantry.

6

BUS RACE

THE TURMOIL CAUSED by the VII rocket attack on Churchill House at the end of the war continued to disrupt Wanstead and Woodford's scheduled bus services. The 10 and 10A double-decker services running between Chigwell and Woodford to the Green Man depot at Leytonstone remained cancelled, leaving only a relief No 20 red double-decker to ply between Wanstead Hospital and Chigwell underground station.

On a fresh Monday morning, just after the 8 o'clock news, Nick wheeled his green Flyer round to the junction of Eagle Lane and Hermon Hill. A 6-mile sprint to Chigwell, he'd decided, was just what the doctor ordered.

"Up early, aren't we?" chided an attractive young female conductor, awaiting her first paying customer. "Hop on and I won't charge you for the bike."

"Some hopes. Any case I'll be at Chigwell station long before you are. Fancy a race?"

"What our Dennis against your push bike? Any time."

The bus driver, having heard this exchange, hopped up into his cab and fired the engine into life. He let in the clutch and the passenger-less 20 Relief to Chigwell rolled forward.

Nick didn't wait for any official starter's flag and flung himself across the Dayton's saddle and began furiously pedalling behind the bus. His front wheel was so close to its rear that he could read the name of the printer who'd produced its 'Ah Bisto' poster. "See you outside Chigwell Station," he called up to the driver as he swung out to overtake, passing the newsagents where he bought his fortnightly copy of *Eagle*.

After passing two deserted request bus stops Nick realised that his main hope in keeping the red monster at bay was London Transport's obligatory white bus stops – where buses had to halt even in the absence of customers. George Lane was one such advantage. The sharp left opposite the modelmakers' shop loomed up. He remembered to leave his pedals at 3 o'clock and 9 o'clock to avoid snagging the granite corner kerbs and leaned hard over. There were no passengers waiting by the stop outside the underground station.

Nick went up a cog on the derailleur and, still seated, headed for the junction with the North Circular arterial road connecting Walthamstow and central Ilford. Now he was touching 25mph. But as he approached the busy crossing the traffic lights turned against him and his two-minute advantage was wiped out. He rested on the toe caps of his racing shoes as the No 20 pulled in behind him, letting off its air brakes in mock-derision.

The rush hour traffic streamed relentlessly past, but the lights stayed stubbornly on red. Nick dismounted and without looking back at the bus driver calmly wheeled his green Flyer across the dual carriageway between the traffic, re-mounted and cycled off in the direction of Chigwell, leaving the bus stationery and its crew fuming.

The next stop was Woodford Bridge, with a good chance of passengers waiting at a white bus stop. As he rounded the final bend he was delighted to see an accompanied school group lined up at the stop, awaiting the arrival of the red 20 Relief. He knew a crocodile of excited toddlers would take several minutes to board. Two miles to go and the race was as good as won.

On through light traffic and up Chigwell Rise. Suddenly, out of nowhere, a very muddy agricultural pick-up, towing a highly-varnished horse box, swung out of a side turning in front of him. Nick swore and applied his brakes. Seated alongside the driver was a woman in a yellow head scarf and a small girl wearing a riding hat. On one of the trailer's rear doors was a sign saying 'ONGAR GYMKHANA'. 'Ah hah' thought Nick, 'late for dressage, are we?' and slipped in behind the horse box for a welcome tow all the way to Chigwell Station.

He coasted into the car park, fully three minutes before the red double-decker pulled in behind him. He had treated himself to an ice cream and was leaning against the bike's crossbar. "What kept you?" he asked the driver with a grin.

"Trouble is we never agreed no Rules of Engagement before the start, did we? Seriously lad, you rode a blinder." He chuckled. "There was folk at one request stop in George Lane who must have thought the Tour de France had come to Britain. And as for that 'tow' you got behind the horse box... well done, young man. Fancy a re-match?"

"Any time."

"Well, once a month – of a Saturday - we do a run from The Green Man, Leytonstone to Epping market. It's a sort of shoppers' day out. I reckon it's got to be a good 14 miles, with some nice high-speed sections for you along the Epping New Road, though I'll have to stick to 40 mph."

"Yeah, I'd be up for that. But just give me a bit of warning, will you?"

Back at Eagle Court Nick found a long message from his mother. "Have gone to Mumfords as the Eagle Court grapevine says a consignment of tinned goods arrived yesterday. We might as well stock up, even though I'll have to queue. Will you take the attached list of mourners over to Rozel for your Grandmother to see? It came in the post this morning from the undertakers. It will be nice for her to have a record of who attended. Love Mother xx PS: Have arranged to meet your Aunt Denise in London on Monday."

Before setting off for Rozel Nick decided to spend half-an-hour 'hoard hunting' as his father's chest of drawers had been such a rich source before. The cabinet was in a 30s-style maple veneer, part of a suite which the newly-weds had purchased at Heals. He found no cash concealed inside the rolled silk ties, in the large leather cuff link box or between the neatly-ironed Turnbull & Asser shirts. But there was a second bundle of socks – woollen this time – lurking at the very back. Fifteen in total. He laid them out on his mother's bed and knew at once from their feel that there was paper inside. The final tally was £300. Nick called Matt's house to give him the good news but his mother said he was out on a nature ramble in Epping Forest with Moira. "Could you say I rang and tell him that my mother is going to London for the day on Monday?"

Nick cycled across Wanstead to The Green and walked up Rozel's front path. He fished the undertakers' list of attendees from his pannier and let himself in. He found Grandma Belle crouched over the *Sporting Times* at the kitchen table.

"Perfect timing, Nicholas. You can ring today's bets through to my bookmaker; then fix me up with a drop of nose paint, will you dear – even though it's not quite 12?" She handed him a slip of paper.

On his return he read out her racing choices. "'Bumble Bee' 'That's-a-Plenty' and 'Fallingwater'. 'That's-a-Plenty' is a jazz number by Freddie Randall. All with Deveraux up?"

"Of course!"

"But the other day you described him as a rank outsider."

"And so he is. But the odds should be good. Fancy going 50:50?"

"Rather." Nick felt honoured as this was the first time his grandmother had ever offered him a bet. "How much?"

"Can you afford 10 shillings?"

"I should think so. Will that be enough?"

"Certainly. Tell him we want a £1 win treble on these three. The beauty of the treble, you see, is that the odds pile up with each win." She swivelled the racing paper round. "At this morning's odds, if young Mr Deveraux brings 'em all home, we'll get odds of 180-to-one."

Nick checked the scribbled list. "The third one's interesting too" he observed. "That's the name of a famous architectural landmark in America: a house, designed for a millionaire by Frank Lloyd Wright, over a waterfall. I'll ring 'em through then get you your drink."

Five minutes later Nick returned to the kitchen with Grandma Belle's lunchtime cocktail in its usual glass. He placed the undertakers' attendance list beside it. "Mother says she thought you'd like to see who came to the funeral."

The card was headed:

Joint Funeral Service for
Mr Harold J. Bostock (1870-1944)
& Mr Alan H.E. Jones (1889-1944),
St Mary's Parish Church, Wanstead.

She absent-mindedly slid it under her racing paper. "Thank you, dear. Seems a funny name to give a racehorse, don't you think?"

"What's that?"

"Falling in the water."

"No Grandma… it's 'Fallingwater!'"

"I see." But she didn't.

* * *

It was just after noon when Nick sauntered down The Green towards the traffic junction. Odds of 180-to-one would net him another £90. There was no chance of the Plessey mob being in The George this early for their lunch break. As he was locking his bike to a lamp post, he saw the dishevelled figure of the Grumpy Groundsman approaching, pushing his bike which obviously had a punctured front tyre.

"Lawks a mussy, you should've seen 'em last weekend. There was a four-ball mixed competition. If you'd been a fish in The Basin by the 14th you'd 'ave thought it was raining bleedin' Dunlop 65s." Nick made a mental note to try to persuade Matt to accompany him on one of his Sunday-morning swims.

"Trouble is them young Turks 'ave got more money than sense. The club's car park looked like Jack Barclay's Showroom, it did!"

The groundsman shuffled off in the direction of Masons Cycle Shop and Nick took shelter in The George. No customers in the saloon bar; just Raj polishing glasses. Placing the drink in front of Nick the Indian manager told him: "I've got a letter for you."

"Oh yes?"

The manager took a sealed blue envelope from a shelf behind the bar and handed it to him. Inside was a sepia postcard. It showed the iconic still from Howard Hughes' *The Outlaw*. Sprawled across some hay, a sultry Jane Russell as good as bared all. Nestling between her legs was a grey .45 colt revolver. On the reverse, Doreen's hand-written message read: "Would you like to come over to my place for lunch on Sunday? I'll meet you

24

outside the Gants Hill Odeon at 1 o'clock. Just leave a message with Raj if you can't make it. Dx"

As there was no sign of the Plessey girls Nick opted to cycle back to Eagle Court, using an indirect network of side roads offering some short sharp climbs. He unlocked his bike and as he wheeled it past the opened gates of the Plessey plant, an unmarked blue box-sided lorry was backing out. A corner of its sheeted load had been blown back by a gust of wind, revealing 8 large white plywood cases in two rows. All had 'A-P D' stencilled on them, with an upright wine glass showing the correct way they should be stacked. On his short hill climbs though Wanstead's back streets Nick reflected on what A-P D might stand for. Certainly not 'Christmas Decorations'.

When he got back to the flat Nick found his mother in the kitchen staring at a mountain of unmarked tins. "They were cheap enough, but the trouble is it doesn't say what's in them."

"So, you may have bought two dozen cans of cat food!"

"Somehow, I doubt it. More likely to be Canadian baked beans, I'd say. The place is still in an awful mess, Nick. Mr Mumford and the girls have been cleaning up debris for days."

"Really?"

"There's still broken glass everywhere. One whole display window is going to have to be replaced and poor Mr Mumford's lovely bacon slicer is ruined. All his regular customers were being most understanding. So how was your grandmother?"

"Fine. We're doing a small joint-wager at Kempton Park this afternoon."

"Gambling? I'm not sure I approve, Nicholas."

"It's only ten bob, mum. And if our three runners all come in first, we stand to collect £180. And my share will be going straight into the sweet tin in the pantry."

"I'll believe that when I see it. Once I've stored these items, I want to have a word with you about that sweet tin."

Nick adopted a 'butter-wouldn't-melt-in-my-mouth' response'. "Sweet tin?"

"Yes. The Quality Street sweet tin in the pantry. Our cash reserves appear to be growing rather than shrinking. I'm sure the Chancellor of the Exchequer would like to know how you've achieved that."

"Err, well Matt and I have had one or two little investments that have paid off."

"Such as?"

"Err such as my golf ball recycling operation."

"There was £670 in the tin when I went to get some cash out to pay Mumfords this morning. Yet last week it stood at around £300. Surely you haven't sold *that* many golf balls?"

"Oh, I forgot. Father's set of Henry Cotton golf clubs. Matt helped me to get rid of them."

"But they weren't yours to SELL, Nick! Don't you understand: they're part of The Estate!? Uncle Vivian will have kittens if he finds out. So where else did the money in the tin come from?"

"Just a small amount of cash. All in old £5 notes."

"Where?"

"Hidden in some of father's silk socks." Mimi shook her head in disbelief. "And now you've taken up gambling!"

"You know, we really should think about security. It's not very smart having so much cash in a sweet tin in the pantry."

"Well, we certainly can't open an account with Westminster Bank, that's for sure. Uncle Vivian's pleading of my poverty seems to have fallen on deaf ears. Where do you suggest we hide it?"

"In the coal bunker? I'll get Mr Parker the caretaker to fit a mortice lock to the front door."

7

AUSTRALIA HOUSE

NICK WAS GIVING an extra lustre to the Reynolds 531 tubing on the green Flyer in the garage, after its convincing win against London Transport's sluggish No 20 relief service to Chigwell, when he sensed he was being watched. His mother was standing in the opened doorway, dressed 'to the nines' as if off to Ascot. A summer frock with a matching jacket. Even a hat! She gazed around the garage's re-configured interior which now resembled a cycle shop: spare tyres and tubes, discarded mudguards and several French posters of Tour de France riders.

"Why exactly are you transforming our garage into a branch of Mason's?"

"I'm not. Just getting rid of some of father's junk. So where are you off to dressed up like that, Mother?" he teased. "Buckingham Palace?"

Ignoring his Smart Alec question and down to earth with a bump she replied: "And what's become of your father's Rover?"

He didn't look up but applied more polish. "Being serviced."

"I see", she said rather frigidly. "Well, "I'm off to meet Denise. I might not be back until late so I've left you an egg and ham salad in the fridge."

"You take care, now."

Denise was Nick's mother's younger sister. Born in England after the Pacquays escaped from Belgium, she had married Tommy, a talented graphic designer, and settled in south London. Somehow the north-south divide made their meetings rare – and Alan and Tommy's diametrically-opposed political positions didn't help. But this was important. Tommy was away at a trade union conference in Macclesfield. And Mimi urgently needed a second opinion after spotting an advertisement in the *Sunday Express* about a government-sponsored scheme for war orphans.

The none-too-informative announcement was headed
'ASSISTED PASSAGES TO AUSTRALIA.'
Their London rendezvous was not their usual spot outside the main entrance to Dickens & Jones, but Trafalgar Square. They met beside Nelson's column at 11.30 am. A few desultory remnants of the VE celebrations remained, but the surviving red and blue buntings draped around the lions at the base of the column indicated that General Election fever was now in the air.

Denise had already arrived. Sitting on a bench near the fountains, Mimi handed her a large manilla envelope marked HIGH COMMISSION OF AUSTRALIA. "Our appointment is with a Mr Codrington at 12 noon. He told me on the 'phone our interview would take about half-an-hour."

"Does Nick know you're here?"

"No fear! I told him we were going to do a bit of shopping in the sales." They crossed the road and entered the lofty marble-clad portals of Australia House. Approaching the reception desk Mimi whispered to her sister: "You do the talking will you Den? I'm too nervous."

Denise took the envelope's covering letter and walked up to the desk. She returned after two minutes. "We have to go up in the lift to the third floor to see Mr Codrington."

The English visitors made their way to the lifts. They stepped into an empty lift car and the bronze and glass doors slid shut. Denise pressed '3' and they were silently carried upwards. When the doors opened a young be-spectacled secretary, clutching some files, was waiting to greet them. "Please follow me." A side window showed a panoramic view of Trafalgar Square.

The secretary stopped before a door marked 3/17 EMIGRATION and opened it. It revealed a busy open-planned office with more than a dozen clerks at work. The girl led them across the space to a dark polished door bearing a small brass plate announcing J.J. CODRINGTON. She knocked and opened it.

Seated behind a huge desk in the window on the far side was a balding man in his 50s, wearing a black jacket and black-and-grey striped trousers. It wasn't exactly a cluttered desk.

"Mrs Thomas and Mrs Jones," the girl announced.

He stood and greeted them in a broad Australian accent. "G'day ladies. Come and take a seat. Thank you, Amanda."

The walls of his palatial office – it could easily have accommodated five Mr Codringtons – were lined with coloured aerial photographs of the Australian countryside and famous city landmarks. On either side of Mr Codrington's panoramic view of Trafalgar Square and its fountains were framed portraits of the British King and Queen and the Governor General of Australia, Lord Slim of Burma wearing his distinctive Ghurkha hat.

Denise and Mimi sat dutifully before the official's desk. He folded his hands. He had done this thing a dozen times and was word-perfect in just what the Assisted Passages to Australia system offered. Clearing his throat – and making a miniscule adjustment to the ruler set below his leather-cornered desk blotter - he began: "Right ladies. I assume you have read and digested the contents of the brochure you were sent?"

"We have," answered Denise.

He checked one of the papers Amanda had left on his desk and turned to Mimi. "Mrs Jones: Nicholas is your son, I believe?"

Opening her mouth for the first time since setting foot in Australia House, Mimi meekly replied: "Yes he is."

"In good health?"

"Very good. He's very athletic too."

"Excellent. No underlying medical conditions?"

"None".

Codrington gave a nod of satisfaction and struck through a line in one of the documents in front of him. "Then a medical examination will be unnecessary." Denise gave Mimi an old-fashioned look, slightly raising her eyebrows.

Codrington turned to his document's second page. "Right. School examinations. Has your son sat his O or A Levels yet?"

"He's due to sit them shortly. He's done his 'Mocks'".

"And his chosen subjects?"

Mimi thought for a moment. "Maths, English and Art. He's also pretty fluent in French."

The Australia House Jobsworth nodded and closed his file. It looked as if their 'interview' was drawing to a close. "Well, subject to Nicholas passing in those subjects – and pending receipt of a letter from your GP vis-à-vis inoculations – I think I can safely say that we will be able to accommodate your son on one of our trips in the New Year. At the moment we're going to Perth. There are normally 25-30 youngsters in each party, which is accompanied by an experienced chaperone." He glanced down again at his papers as the door opened and Amanda reappeared. "I've still got three vacancies on the *SS Perth Horizon*, which is due to sail from Tilbury next March. Why don't I pencil him in there?"

Mimi looked at Denise. The question sounded like a death sentence and she just stared down at the folded hands in her lap. Denise answered brightly: "What a good idea!"

"Yes Amanda?" asked Mr Codrington expectantly.

"Your luncheon appointment in Whitehall with the Minister, sir. It's almost quarter-to-one."

Mr Codrington stood up. "Ladies – I do apologise: duty calls. Amanda will show you out." Picking up a pair of leather gloves and collecting a black trilby hat from a hatstand by the door, the Emigration Official departed. Amanda escorted the two shell-shocked visitors to the lift and left. Their interview had lasted 12 minutes.

They rode down in silence, though Denise could see that her sister was close to tears. In the marble-lined hall she whispered: "Well that wasn't too bad, was it?"

"Too bad? Too BAD! I feel like I've just sold him into slavery!"

They stood in the sunshine, both stunned. Denise decided to cheer her sister up. "Let's go to Dickens & Jones by taxi. I'll pay."

Twenty minutes later the two were settled at a window table in the department store's Restaurant. Tea and scones were ordered. Sensing her sister's disappointment over their brief session at Australia House, Denise decided that all Australian topics were off-limits. But Mimi had other ideas.

"I didn't like his smug attitude one little bit. After all, we were there to discuss my son's future on the other side of the world. Yet it was all over in under 20 minutes - just so he could toddle off for a free lunch!"

Denise gave a giggle and whispered in French to her sister: "Don't look now but that old battle axe at the next table looks as if she's got a stuffed parrot stuck on her hat!"

Mimi glanced round and chuckled with amusement, replying in French: "D'you think she's been visiting Regent Park Zoo?"

"Either that or there's a pet shop nearby with a closing down sale!" Mimi spluttered scone crumbs into her teacup and began crying with laughter.

The parrot-hat lady settled her bill, arose and swept indignantly past Denise and Mimi, uttering, in an audible stage whisper as she strode past: "*Bon jour, mesdames!*"

Back at Eagle Court Nick's mother appeared in very subdued form at around 7.00 pm. There was a noticeable absence of any big Dickens & Jones bags. She said she didn't want any supper as she had a headache. It was to be an egg and ham salad for one and an early night.

8

MISGIVINGS

MIMI TOOK THE BUS to Wanstead, though it was not to visit her mother-in-law.

She first paid a brief visit to the bright white Roman Catholic church of St Theresa that faced the east side of The Green. There was no service in progress and the only two nuns in sight were young novices arranging fresh flowers on the altar. From the top of the nearby pulpit, a well-fed Mother Superior, as large as Margaret Rutherford, pretended to polish the brass shade of the reading light – while monitoring their progress.

Had a priest been in attendance Mimi would certainly have gone to Confession, but a chalked notice beside the confessional box read: 'NEXT CONFESSIONALS – SATURDAY'. She genuflected at the back of the church and left.

Next door was the surgery of their family doctor, Henry O'Toole. Her appointment was for 10.30 am and she was shown into his consulting room promptly.

"And what seems to be the problem, Mimi?"

"It's not me, doctor. I've come about Nicholas." She laid the large manilla envelope on his desk. "He's off to Australia and I've been told to get you to sign these confirmations that he's currently inoculated against various diseases." She attempted to make the whole thing as matter-of-fact as possible. But inwardly she was petrified.

"Australia? But I thought he was just about to sit his 'O' levels? At Alan's funeral he told me he wanted to train to be a structural engineer."

Mimi gazed down at her lap. "There's been a slight change of plan."

"Your idea?"

She nodded. "I saw an advertisement in the *Sunday Express*."

"For what exactly?"

After a long pause: "I've enrolled him on the government's Assisted Passages scheme. The one that sends war orphans to Australia for £10." Mimi was close to crying.

The doctor replaced the cap of his fountain pen and put it down on the blotter, but made no attempt to look inside the big brown envelope. "Australia?" Then after a long pause: "Mimi – that's an awfully long way away, you know. Half the circumference of the globe almost. Leaving you all on your own at Eagle Court?"

She nodded. "I know. I know." She awaited more sympathy, but none was forthcoming. He'd not even asked if she had discussed this life-changing plan with her son.

"Of course, I'll confirm that Nicholas has had all the necessary inoculations and so forth for foreign travelling… but I'd urge you to think very carefully before it's too late."

"I will" she replied meekly, disappointed by her doctor's lack of support. She stood up and accepted his limp handshake, leaving without saying another word. From the surgery Mimi walked diagonally across The Green (holding back her tears) to pay a short courtesy call on her Mother-in-Law, with the doctor's bland cautionary words 'before it's too late' ringing in her ears.

9

DAGENHAM DIVA

DOREEN THE CHARGEHAND met him outside the Gants Hill Odeon on the dot of 1.00 pm. She was wearing a flowing summery dress with prints of poppies and a swooping neckline almost as revealing as Jane Russell's blouse. Without her signature turban she looked altogether different. More feminine. He climbed off his bike, unclipped his jeans and followed her down a cobbled alleyway which ran behind the big cinema. He padlocked the Dayton to a lamp post as she indicated a small entrance door and he followed her inside, taking two half-bottles of wine from the bike's pannier.

They climbed a narrow wooden staircase, eventually arriving on the third floor, in front of her flat's front door, oak-panelled but un-numbered. A Yale lock opened to reveal a compact attic space, tidy and tastefully furnished in a sort of bohemian Art Nouveau style. He recognised a print of *The Kiss* by Gustav Klimt, showing embracing lovers: an appropriate picture for a 'love nest' he thought. A narrow door ajar gave a tantalising glimpse of her bedroom with a divan, on which a midnight blue negligee was laid.

The tiny bedroom's single leaded casement looked out onto Gants Hill Gardens, crowded with Sunday strollers. She set the wine bottles down on a small gate-leg table laid for two. "I tell you Nick, after working underground for a whole week it's an absolute joy to come back here."

"I bet it is. Want me to uncork the wine?"

"Yes please, sweetie." She put on an apron, handed him a corkscrew and moved towards a narrow galley, no bigger than you'd find on a canal barge. To save space the connecting door with the living room wasn't hinged but hung on runners. "Right, it shouldn't be long – say 20 minutes – 'it' being roast leg of lamb, onion sauce, new potatoes and green runner beans. Followed by fresh fruit salad."

"Delicious." He lifted his glass. "Cheers."

"I say," she commented after a sip, "that's a bit special isn't it?"

"Sauterne. There's another 22 where that came from."

"How come?"

"I'm subtly liquidating my late father's assets; converting them into cash to support my mother. She'll get a State Widow's pension, of course. Eventually. But as the silly old fool died Intestate we're trying to turn as much as possible of his assets into cash to bolster her housekeeping."

She moved to the galley. "And how was Jane Russell?"

"Glorious."

"Did she bare all?"

"A good 65 per cent I'd say, though I'm something of a novice in that department."

"You DO surprise me." Doreen frothed up the gravy with a whisk. "That Howard Hughes was a pervy devil and no mistake."

"Really?

"So cinemagoers would get a good eyeful of her ample cleavage he'd even designed a special 'uplift' bra for her for that hay loft scene. But the puritanical Hays Office made him cut it out. So she finished up padding her original bra with Kleenex tissues." Doreen gave a snigger. "You've certainly come to the right address for smutty trivia, mate!"

"Are you planning to stay on at Plesseys in Wanstead?"

"For as long as I can. The money's good: 12/6 a week. But the rumour is that they're going to wind it all down by Christmas."

"Who's 'they'?"

"The ministry big wigs who hand out the contracts. We call them 'The Suits'"

"For Christmas decorations?"

She smiled as she brought the lamb joint to the table. "Something like that. So, tell me Nick: how old are you exactly?"

"Nearly 16."

"I said 'exactly'."

"Fifteen years and 8 months."

Having completed serving them both, she took another generous swig of the white wine and sat down. After slowly savouring her cooking with satisfaction she shook her head thoughtfully and quietly announced: "Mmmm... well that does slightly complicate matters."

"How so?"

"Not heard of the age of consent?"

"Sort of."

She slowly chewed a piece of lamb before washing it down with the last of her wine. Nick refilled her glass. "Strictly speaking - and I'm just being hypothetical here, you understand - if thoughts of hanky-panky come to mind, it's officially off-limits for another four months, I'm afraid." Demurely, she placed her knife and fork down on the plate and gave him an angelic smile.

"Rats!"

She let him 'stew' for a full 30 seconds and then gave one of the raucous laughs he'd heard in The George. "But I'm all for a bit of law-breaking if you are!"

"Rather! So have you always lived alone, Doreen? You seem such a gregarious person".

"I like it here. It's my own private sanctuary. I tried sharing but it didn't work. He was a bookie's runner down Dagenham Dogs - my favourite course. Initially it was fine; then he started scrounging; and before I knew it, I was feeding a lodger who didn't contribute a brass farthing. He always was 'a wide runner'. She squeezed Nick's thigh through his jeans. "Give me 'a railer' every night! So I kicked the bastard out and got the locks changed."

"So where is he now – this 'wide runner'?" Even with the protection of a changed lock, Nick was in no mood to argue with one of her ex-lovers.

"Jaywick Sands."

"Sounds exotic. Where's that? Cornwall?"

"Essex. Next door to Clacton. Believe me, mate, it's the tips. Back in the 30s it started life as an idyllic seaside resort for East Enders. There were rows of quaint little timber bungalows. The fellow who developed the land obviously had a thing about flash motors, as every street is named after a classic model: Wolseley

Avenue, Daimler Way, Buick Close." She shook her head sorrowfully. "Not any longer. It's a cess pit full of low-life detritus, pimps and strutting, hard-line druggies with big Alsatians." She picked up their two empty plates. "Ready for pudding – or shall we go to bed?"

"Bed!"

They sat nervously on the edge of the bed. Doreen broke the ice with a joke: "How do you get an Essex girl into bed?" Nick shook his head.

"Piece of cake!" Placing a hand on his thigh she whispered: "Right, tell me: did you ever go to ballroom dancing classes when you were young?"

"Only twice. Mrs Bailey's Tap & Dance Academy. I didn't like it. It was around the time I'd discovered trad jazz. Victor Sylvester and Freddie Randall made odd bed fellows."

"I see. Well the reason I ask is because your teacher will probably have used the term 'leading' – meaning the male dancer has to guide his partner."

"Yes, I think I remember that. She had a chart on the wall with our feet marked as black blobs."

Doreen gave a girlish giggle and turned away from him, lifting her blouse to reveal a black brassiere strap. "Un-hook me would you sweetie?"

She turned to face him, clasping her arms tight around her unsupported bosom. Then she released her crossed arms. "You like?"

"Mmm I like a lot!"

"Right, well here's one piece of advice from those ballroom dancing classes: I'll lead… you follow!"

"OK, but as you'll have guessed I'm no expert. It's all 'unchartered territory' to me, I'm afraid."

"Yes, I'd rather gathered that."

"So can you give me an idea of how long it goes on for?"

She placed her empty glass on the floor, causing her huge breasts to swing free. "As long as you like, sweetie. All night if necessary."

"All night?"

"Have you heard of an ancient Indian sex manual called the *Kama Sutra*?"

"No."

"I'll lend you my copy. In that book the author lists 94 different positions…"

"For what?"

"Doing it, stupid. Now let's get those jeans of yours off so the dog can see the rabbit."

Nick heard the metallic click of his flies being slowly unzipped. "And remember: I'll lead."

10

STORM CLOUDS

"SO WHERE WERE *you* yesterday?" Doreen asked rather truculently when they met up next in the bar of The George (Matt and Moira were at the cinema next door). Her hands were on her hips.

"Mum didn't get back 'til late and said she had a headache. So, I turned in early. Sorry."

She went a little 'girlie' on him as 19 pairs of eyes up at the bar awaited the next move in this tense chess game.

"Sorry."

"You've said that once already. So why did your mother need to go to London?"

"Search me. The odd thing is she didn't buy anything. Anything at all. That's virtually unheard of in our household. She met her sister and they usually buy stuff in Dickens & Jones as if it was going out of fashion." Doreen remained standing, as if not wholly convinced by his explanation. She traced a finger across the velvet banquette. "I wasn't going to tell you this… but…"

"But?"

"I missed you on Sunday night after you'd gone."

He placed his hand gently on hers. "Same here."

"Truly?"

"Truly."

She looked up at the clock over the bar. "Shit!"

"What's up?"

"Our bus goes in eight minutes and I'm about to blub. Shit, shit, shit!"

Jumping up Doreen pulled her white cotton coat straight. "Come on ladies, let's be having you!" She leaned forward and kissed him on the forehead. Then without looking back she followed the last of the Plessey workers out into the street.

* * *

Promptly at 5 o'clock the following day Nick was sat in his usual corner seat in The George. Today, after a brief visit to his grandmother's house he was counting his share of their 'Deveraux Treble' which had netted them £180. He decided he would donate 50% of his winnings to the Quality Street kitty, despite his mother's cutting remarks about gambling. Used £1 and 10 shilling notes lay in piles in front of him on the table.

"Hello, so where did all that come from? Littlewoods come up for you?" Doreen – now back in full truculent Essex girl mode – stood in front of him.

"On the nags yesterday."

"I didn't know you studied form."

"I don't. It's my Grandmother – you know, the old lady who lives up the road from your plant. Studies *Sporting Life* every morning over breakfast. We had a three-horse accumulator come up at Kempton."

"Well, she must be good. I'd like to meet her." Then after a pause the chargehand added: "On second thoughts that's not such a good idea, seeing as we're almost 'an item'. Nevertheless, I think you could at least buy all the girls a drink." Without waiting for Nick's acquiescence, she called across to Raj: "Set 'em up for the girls, Raj love. And I'll have one of your Pimms Fruit Salad specials."

Matt and Moira were once again absent: Matt was doing revision for his legal examinations and Moira was on a training course at Bearman's department store. Nick decided to face the music alone: his 'now or never' moment had arrived. He'd rather face the music here in The George than back in Doreen's garret. If they came to blows Les Girls would probably tear them apart.

Now it was his turn to trace imaginary patterns in the velvet. "If you must know, on Monday my mother and her sister went up to London to a meeting at Australia House." He paused. "The Emigration Department."

Genuinely baffled by this news Doreen asked: "So is your aunt thinking of emigrating to Australia?"

"Err no, not that I know of."

"Then it's your mum. Now that she's widowed, she wants to start a new life 'down under'?"

This time Nick couldn't even bring himself to speak. He just shook his head slowly.

The penny finally dropped. "You? It's YOU! They're sending YOU off to bloody Australia?"

"It's what's known as their 'Assisted Passages scheme'. It's been set up to assist war orphans where surviving spouses are struggling to make ends meet. I haven't been given the full itinerary yet but I'll be sailing from Tilbury Docks." Doreen's hands were now on her hips, Southend fish wife style.

"So, they've reintroduced Transportation to The Colonies have they?" she announced in a loud voice. "First I'VE heard of it. And I read the *Daily Mirror* every day, don't I Jan?" Aware that her silent 'crew' had picked up most of this heated exchange, Doreen delivered the coup de grace: "And where'll you be going to get fitted for your leg iron – DOLCIS?" Nick remained seated on the banquette. He was pretty sure if he got up and approached her she'd take a swing at him.

The Plessey girls finished their drinks and nervously filed out as Raj held the big entrance door open for them. "Don't forget ladies – clean head scarves this Friday. We've got 'The Suits' coming." In the entrance lobby a group of five, all ashen-faced, stared back like a Greek chorus.

"Will you come and see me off at Tilbury?"

"No, I most certainly will NOT! Come on girls – Doug's got the bus outside. Let's make an early night of it, shall we?" It was a truly theatrical exit.

11

TILBURY

DOCTOR JOHN GRAY, one of Mimi's neighbours in Eagle Court, had generously offered to take her and Nick to Tilbury for her son's departure for Australia. It was 5.30 am, on a bitingly cold March morning, when he brought his maroon and black Ford Granada around to the front of the building. Nick's black leather-bound cabin trunk slipped snugly into the car's boot. The roads were empty and they made good time. Mimi and the doctor chatted away in the front seats, while Nick still nursed the wounds from his humiliating rejection by Doreen in The George.

"All right there in the back, young man?" the jovial doctor enquired looking in the rear-view mirror.

"Fine thanks, Doctor."

"And remember, whatever you do don't denigrate the aborigines like the Aussies do. Those natives are really smart people. Very fine trackers too. It's said they can trace lost cattle just by studying hoof prints in the desert sand. And any way, they were there first!"

The port of Tilbury, at the easternmost end of the Thames estuary, was not the frenetic hive of maritime activity Nick had expected. It still bore its war decorations proudly: camouflage, naval codes whitewashed on shed walls and a total absence of any commercial posters. Incongruously, a single line of mint-condition American Willys jeeps, complete with brilliant white five-pointed stars on their bonnets, was forlornly parked in front of a warehouse as if they had missed the last transport out for Normandy. None of the tall dockside cranes were in action.

Nick and Dr Gray jointly carried the cabin trunk down to the dockside, beside which the huge Blue Line vessel sat moored. A steward handed Nick a receipt and two deckhands carried his trunk aboard *SS Perth Horizon*.

Whose heart could fail to be uplifted by this 49,000-ton ocean-going leviathan that was to transport them half-way round the world? But right at that minute Nick would rather have been at home in bed at Eagle Court. Or, even better, snuggled into Doreen's ample bosom in her Gants Hill garret.

As if to break his reverie the ship let out the first of a series of exclamatory blasts on its steam horn. This brought riotous cheers from the assembled well-wishers up on Tilbury's visitors' gallery, followed by a volley of red, white and blue paper streamers. More blasts on the steam horn. In the half-dark Nick hadn't realised that there were so many people up there, patiently waiting to give the big ship a royal send-off. This was like Wembley after a Cup Final. A human wall of well-wishers.

John Gray simultaneously shook Nick firmly by the hand and placed a bear-like palm reassuringly on his shoulder. Nick embraced his mother, swallowed hard and then trudged up the gangplank without looking back. He knew she was crying; to have even glanced back would have distressed her more.

The passage of *Perth Horizon* down the Tilbury Estuary was slow and without incident. The passengers – both the young emigrants and adult tourists – soon tired of gazing at sugar refineries and scrap metal yards. Nick sauntered below deck to find his cabin and make sure his giant cabin trunk (once used by his Uncle Bob when on leave from Colombo) had been safely stowed away by one of the stewards.

The Perth contingent, he learned, had six adjoining cabins, each with four bunk beds. Being an early visitor Nick managed to 'bag' a bottom bunk, marking it with his overcoat. There was no sign of the other three occupants.

Standing in the cabin's opened doorway was an attractive blonde-haired young woman in her mid-20s holding a clip board, who he initially took to be one of the ship's stewardesses. "Good morning" she said cheerily. "May I have your name?"

"Nicholas Jones."

"Hello Nicholas. I'm Stephenie, your chaperone for the trip down to Perth. I'll be with you all the way and I'll come on the coach transfer to Hollow Tree Farm. Lunch is always at 1.00 pm sharp in the Ballroom on Deck 3 and it's normally signalled by a gong on the PA system. If there's anything you need – at any hour – I'm in Cabin 62 which is at the end of this row."

"So have you done this before?"

"This is my second tour. You'll love it."

"And how will you get back to England?"

"Same ship, same route but I don't have to do any chaperoning – so I can put my feet up, read a good book and enjoy a glass of wine." Nick decided he could easily take to this plain-speaking young woman.

"Can you tell me if there's a gym on this ship, Stephenie?"

"Yes there is. And I'm told its very well equipped." She flipped over the top sheet on her clip board." Deck 1; for'ard." She giggled. "Which I gather means 'the sharp end'.

12

COLONEL NEWMAN VC

AN HOUR AFTER lunch on the second day out of Tilbury and *Perth Horizon* was making its stately passage south down the French coastline, cruising at 30 knots. Passengers began drifting into the ballroom, not entirely sure of what to expect from what the handbills they'd found on their breakfast tables had simply announced as:

"A TALK BY COLONEL CHARLES NEWMAN VC."

Seated behind a table on the Ballroom's stage were the ship's skipper, the dapper Captain Urquhart and a tall grey-haired civilian in a smart grey houndstooth suit. On the left-hand lapel of his jacket was a maroon and blue 'badge bar' – signifying the position that a military honour would be worn on ceremonial occasions.

The skipper rose. "In approximately half-an-hour we shall be sailing due south along the French Loire region's coastline, down towards Gibraltar, passing the mouth of the St Nazaire Estuary.

"Older passengers may possibly be familiar with a famous amphibious operation of the last war known as the Battle of St Nazaire. It is my great pleasure to tell you that the leader of that operation, Colonel Charles Newman, is seated beside me.

Newman stood. Rangy, with a commanding presence, he adjusted the knot of his striped military tie. "One small apology is the absence of what I believe are today termed 'visual aids': charts and aerial photos and such like. We only learned 24 hours ago that Colonel Newman was travelling with us, bound for an international conference in Cape Town. So, the story you are about to hear will just be in his own words. Ladies and gentlemen: Colonel Newman."

The old soldier coughed and consulted his watch. "Right – twenty-two minutes. Then I suggest we go on deck." He glanced down at Tom Urquhart. "The skipper here says that the ship's horn will tell us when we're approaching the mouth of the estuary. Port side.

""Operation Chariot'. Not entirely sure why they called it that. The war house box-wallahs loved dreaming up improbable names for military operations. 'Operation Short Straw' would have been nearer the mark. It seems I got the job on the recommendation of Admiral Louis Mountbatten. I take my hat off to his strategic planners; they were certainly spot on with 'Chariot'. Hobbling *Bismark* and *Tirpitz* by denying them the Normandie dry dock for essential repairs effectively relegated them to floating museums for the rest of the war.

"The object of the exercise, ladies and gentlemen, was for a heavily-disguised maritime raiding party to sail up the St Nazaire estuary and destroy its huge inland dry dock where, pre-war, the *Normandie* trans-Atlantic liner had been built. At 79,000 tons this was the pride of the French merchant service. When it was completed in 1932 *Normandie* enjoyed the protection of the largest dry dock in the world.

"Prime Minister Churchill's experts had told him that if the dry dock could be put out of use, the German navy would have no dockyard capable of accommodating and repairing *Bizmark* or *Tirpitz*, the enemy's two invincible battle cruisers which then ruled the Atlantic, destroying priceless merchant shipping convoys of food and raw materials from north America with impunity.

"Rather surprisingly both the SOE and the Navy turned the job down. Even the RAF declined to get involved (they'd clearly never heard of Professor Barnes-Wallis). So it fell to me to form a task force, mainly of Commandos. I seem to recall it was planned remarkably quickly – by inter-service standards that is; probably less than a year. We trained for three weeks at the Royal Marines' base in Devon. Two weeks in fatigues and the last week in our fishermen's outfits." He gave a fond chuckle of remembrance. "The locals must have thought we were rehearsing for *The Pirates of Penzance*".

"One hundred and seventy-eight survived the operation; 434 were captured or killed. There were 20 vessels in our secret flotilla, led by an old WW1 Warhorse *HMS Campbelltown*, disguised with German naval markings. It was stacked with 4 tons of high explosives in her bows, intended to detonate on impact. At least that's what they told us! We knew we faced a huge reception committee as the Germans prized this unique naval installation, keeping a garrison of around 6000 on permanent alert. There was just over 600 of us, all disguised as Breton fishermen.

"We launched the unmanned destroyer which crashed into the docks' gates, but the impact failed to detonate its hidden 'bomb'. The garrison turned out in force and a long fire fight ensued (we only had light arms and grenades). Cordite filled the air. This was text book street fighting just like we'd rehearsed it at Bickley, but we were out-gunned by 10:1. I was all for making a swift retreat under cover of darkness. I'd even convinced myself we could make it on foot to Portugal.

"Fortunately, I was outvoted and so I had to run up the white flag. I finished up in Spangenberg Castle in the Hesse. Four hours after our official surrender the dear old *Campbelltown* finally decided to detonate, blowing both the dry docks' gates off." With a sigh, the old soldier sat down.

Captain Urquhart rose. "Ladies and gentlemen, boys and girls: on your behalf may I say what a privilege it is to hear that from the man who commanded that operation – an operation which even the German High Command – Admiral Doenitz no less – expressed an admiration for because of its sheer audacity." The captain glanced through a porthole. "Right, I see we are now approaching the mouth of the Loire."

"We have one more surprise for you: a quiz. And it has just one answer. Blue Line has agreed that the winner can join me and the Colonel up on the bridge as we pass the estuary's entrance. Right: here's the question: 'Operation Chariot netted the largest number of bravery awards of any single operation in the Second World War'. Would anyone care to say how many medals were won?" Silence was followed by much whispering. "I'll give you a clue: it's in double figures."

"Twenty? No, you've got to go much higher, sir. Thirty-six? No, you're still way under par."

A young father, wearing a Commando tie, raised his hand. "Yes, sir?"

The man hoisted his son onto the chair he'd been sitting in, nudging him encouragingly to call out the answer. The boy looked down sheepishly at his father and then shouted: "89!"

"Is the correct answer," called the captain as the ship's horn sounded. "Right, all hands on deck."

* * *

"Thanks for that riveting description of Operation Chariot this afternoon." Nick nervously addressed a seated Col Newman in the ship's library later. He was engrossed in the contents of a thick manilla file marked 'FOREIGN OFFICE; TOP SECRET'. Newman looked up, smiled and flipped the folder closed, clearly glad of the interruption.

"Are you coming all the way to Perth?" Nick asked.

"Sadly no. I'm only travelling with you as far as Cape Town. HM Government has chosen me to represent them at an international conference on Post-War European Reparation. I was just doing a bit of 'mugging up', so to speak. Won't you take a seat?"

Nick sat opposite the old soldier. "As well as thanking you for the talk, I wanted to present you with a small World War Two souvenir." He reached into his pocket, withdrew a Bryant & May matchbox and placed it in front of the war hero.

Newman picked up the box and rattled it. Then slid out its tray and deposited the lump of shrapnel on the table beside his file. "Shrapnel! So do you collect this stuff?"

"Not really. But that one's a bit special. It's a fragment of the doodle bug that hit a block of flats near where I live in Wanstead."

"'Wanstead' you say? I was at school at Bancrofts."

"I know. With my father, Alan Jones."

"Old Alan, eh? Good golfer, I seem to recall. And he boxed for the school." Newman turned the metal fragment over, inspecting it carefully. "And you want me to have this?"

"Yes please, sir. Perhaps it'll bring you luck in Cape Town."

13

A DEATH AT SEA

THERE WAS AN air of expectation at breakfast as the liner got ever closer to the legendary Rock of Gibraltar, with much talk about the apes. The ginger-haired twins Daisy and Marigold wanted to know if they could feed them.

"Now you're not to be disappointed if we arrive there after dark, as I doubt if the captain will let you youngsters ashore," Stephenie cautioned. "There can be some very undesirable people lurking around on the wharves at night. Gibraltar is very close to Morocco, you know?" She looked at the twins. "You might get kidnapped and finish up in a harem."

"What's a harem, Miss?" one of the twins asked.

"You know: belly dancers and exotic music. You must have seen it in the cinema."

Their steward cleared away the breakfast things and stood beside Stephenie for further orders. She smiled at him. "That's all, thank you Ali. We'll be in for lunch at 1.00 pm." The steward bowed and departed. Steph cast an eye through a porthole. "It's looking a bit chilly out there, so if you go on deck please wear something waterproof. Otherwise, I suggest you read in the Library until you hear the luncheon gong sound. After lunch I'll be taking you through the questions to my Breakfast Quiz. Everyone seemed happy with this announcement except brainy Stephen, who wanted to know more about harems

"Get Nick here to show you how to look it up in *Britanica* in the Library."

Ian, the youngest member of her party, sidled up to Stephenie. "Can't I stay in my cabin?"

"Of course you can, sweetheart. Just make sure the stewards have made up the bunks. Then be back here for lunch at 1 sharp. It's shepherd's pie followed by strawberry ice cream."

Ian sloped off, though his round-shouldered demeanour indicated disillusionment.

Having set up Stephen with a *Britanica* volume Nick was determined to track down any Tour de France features or Giro d'Italia previews.

It was shortly before 12.45 pm when a discordant claxon sound from the loudspeakers echoed throughout the salons and companionways. "MAN OVERBOARD! MAN OVERBOARD!" Then the sound of the vessels huge engines being switched to idling, followed by Captain Urquhart's voice: "Ladies and gentleman, boys and girls. Please remain where you are and don't venture up on deck for the present." Stephen looked quizzically at Nick, who shrugged his shoulders and tried to resume his cycle racing article.

Stephenie appeared by Nick's side. She placed a hand on his shoulder and whispered: "It's Ian. I checked his cabin and its empty, though the steward said he saw him heading up on deck wearing an orange anorak." The ice-cool chaperone appeared shaken. Nick grabbed Steph's hand. "Come on, let's see what's going on."

Perth Horizon was stationary, gently rocking in calm waters. Tom Urquhart was leaning over the bridge rail directing the lowering of one of the liner's lifeboats into the water through a loud-hailer. "Launch Lifeboat Number One!" After its davits were swung out two deck hands – fore and aft – let go of tensioned ropes and the tub fell like a stone onto the water. Four able seamen scrambled down rope ladders and boarded the lifeboat. Initially it moved forward under power; then its engine was cut and the youngest of the crew slowly steered the lifeboat aft, using a single sideways movement of one oar, much as Venetian gondoliers do.

Urquhart raised his megaphone. "Further back, further back!" he urged the crew. Stephenie and Nicholas saw one of his deputies take a place beside him at the rail. He handed the skipper what looked like a child's doll wearing a scarlet crinoline dress. The captain stepped back two or three paces then rushed forward to the rail, at the same time despatching the red 'doll' into the air towards – and beyond – the lifeboat. It was a huge arcing throw that seemed to go on forever. Now the doll was descending, landing in the water a full 50 metres beyond the lifeboat, popping tantalisingly to the surface. Urquhart raised the megaphone to his lips. "Search there!"

The skipper's skilful despatch of the red marker buoy brought back to Nick memories of an amazing 'run out' which he had witnessed in a county cricket match between Middlesex and Surrey at The Oval. In English First Class cricket 'running four' is as risky as it gets; it can be as nerve-racking as baseball run-outs. Dennis Compton and Bill Edrich were knocking the ball all over the ground and it was obvious they were both hungry for centuries. After a massive drive from Edrich, Eric Bedser, fielding at deep long on, raced round, scooped up the ball inches from the boundary rope and returned it with an almighty heft, using the same arcing throw which Urquhart had so expertly employed, into the red leather gloves of the wicket keeper, the ever-dependable Arthur McIntyre. Run out: the bails were off and Bill Edrich just carried on running towards the Surrey pavilion.

The young rating who had been steering the lifeboat needed no command from his captain. Stripping off his shirt he dived deep into the water alongside the marker buoy. After half a minute he emerged breathless and grim-faced. He raised one arm to show the discarded arm of an orange anorak. Stephenie's nails dug into Nick's arm and her head dropped forward. Urquhart gave a long blast on his whistle. Waving one arm he called through the megaphone: "Come back alongside."

The recovery of the lifeboat was as impressive as its launching. Shocked passengers dispersed, leaving the Captain and Stephenie deep in conversation. As Nick stood and watched the lifeboat being hauled back on board, the ship's engines picked up to their normal throbbing, driving the ship forwards again to resume its journey south.

By lunchtime Steph had perked up a little though there were red rings around her eyes. The luncheon's shepherd's pie was consumed largely in silence and it was difficult not a take an occasional glance at Ian's empty place. As the stewards were collecting up the pudding plates the captain appeared on the stage at the end of the Ballroom, his cap under his arm. "There is to be a short Memorial Service in the Ship's Chapel at 3.00 pm."

Glancing across at Stephenie's table he added: "I hope all of you who knew Ian will come along."

The ship's Chapel was surprisingly compact for a liner capable of carrying 700 passengers. A small internal square on A Deck, its walls were simply lined with rectangular panels of maple. A pale blue carpet, edged in dark blue, covered the whole floor. There was a maple-fronted font and lectern but no altar as such: just a table draped with an embroidered altar cloth and a cross. What dramatically stood this simple interior apart was an acid-etched glass depiction, inset into the front of the altar-table, of *The Light of the World*, Pre-Raphaelite Holman Hunt's allegorical image of Christ holding a lantern, knocking on an ivy-covered door. Beneath it a quotation from John 1.5 read: *"The light shines in the darkness, and the darkness can never extinguish it."*

Four rows of seats – rather than pews – accommodated about 80. This afternoon the Chapel was full to capacity, with several late-comers standing in the opened doorway. Even the rating who had dived into the water was there. Captain Urquhart stood alongside the Hollow Tree Farm party, with Stephenie at the other end of the front row.

The service's only hymn was a stirring American evangelical number: *As near the wished-for Port we draw* played on a small electric organ by an elderly lady wearing a trim Panama hat with a black ribbon. She made it sound as if it had come straight from the Mississippi Delta, with a 'wailing' finish Jimmie Smith would have been proud of. The Priest was tall and blonde; no more than 30 years old. He wore a black berretta and a gold-embroidered white silk stole over his black cassock. High up around his chin was a starched white collar. After the opening blessing he told the little congregation that at the end of the service he and the captain would be casting a wreath onto the sea from the stern.

Captain Urquhart rose and walked slowly to the lectern. He had no notes. Folding his hands and studying the leather cover of the Bible in front of him he began: "Thankfully, this is only the third time – in war and peace – that this has happened to me. A young life, with such promising things lying ahead for him. So cruelly cut short. I didn't have the honour of getting to know Ian well, but I know he was well cared for by his chaperone." He paused, looked down at the Bible and concluded: "May his soul rest in peace."

The lady in the Panama closed the organ's lid and the Priest prepared to deliver the closing blessing.

But Nick felt there was more to be said. Much more. He stood, holding his palms out in supplication and looked towards the priest. There was a slight murmur of surprise from some of the grown-ups in the congregation, but the Priest nodded his assent at Nick, who stepped forward staring intently at the Holman Hunt image.

"What Ian did this morning was exceptionally brave. I'm not even half as brave. He missed his mother terribly from the moment we left Tilbury. Like mine, his father was killed in the Blitz. Half-way through the Bay of Biscay, destined for who-knows-what on the far side of the globe, Ian chose to take his leave." Nick shook his head slowly as tears began to fall. "Ian – I salute your bravery." He glanced at the Holman Hunt engraving for a final inspiration. "And remember, Ian: 'The light shines in the darkness'". He sat down and hung his head.

The mourners began filing out, each shaking hands with the priest and the skipper. Nick had composed himself by the time Steph came to collect him. Holding his hand tightly she led him up to Captain Urquhart who shook his hand warmly. "May I say young man that that was an act of immense bravery. Clearly spoken and from the heart." Nick gripped Steph's hand tightly. Her 'Thank you, Captain' helped a bit. "Would you and your chaperone do me the honour of dining at the Captain's Table tonight?"

"We'd love to," Nick replied as he and Stephanie stepped out into the sunshine.

* * *

The sheer size of the ship's principal Dining Room was a revelation to both of them as they stood in the double entrance doorway waiting to be shown to the Captain's table. The silk-clad walls were liberally hung with naval paintings, many depicting successful French conflicts. Portraits of the shipping li line's founders (a branch of the Bugatti dynasty) hung at the far end.

Waiters moved quietly between the tables, most set for either two or four. Urquhart rose to greet his guests. Stephenie was dressed in a pale blue creation with a pearl choker, while Nick sported his Forest School summer blazer. The skipper gestured them to be seated, with Nick in the place of honour at his right hand.

The Dining Room's M'aitre d'Hotel magically appeared at the skipper's side. "Madame, gentlemen. Tonight, we shall be serving vichyssoise soup with parmesan croutons, sole meuniere with asparagus and Pomme de terre a la Dauphinoise, and crème brulée with white currants." He glanced at the captain for a nod of confirmation, handed an embossed Menu Card to Stephenie, and then beckoned to a hovering young wine waiter to approach.

"So how long have you been on this ship?" Steph enquired.

"This will be my twelfth crossing. After Pangbourne and Dartmouth I kept my eyes peeled for the right line to join. Cunard and P&O both had long waiting lists. I didn't want to steal the Colonel's thunder yesterday, but I briefly served on the ill-fated *Normandie*. What a ship!" He looked up at the dining room's ceiling. "To start with, her Dining Room was four deck levels high. And amongst its exotic wall decorations were huge long mirrors edged with Lalique glass. I don't know whether it was a bit of 'public relations bluster' but we were told to tell passengers that the Dining Room was longer than Versailles' Hall of Mirrors!"

The lady who had played the organ in the chapel magically appeared at the captain's side as the soup dishes were being removed. The captain introduced her as Miss Fernside.

"Excuse the intrusion, Captain, but are there any special requests your guests would like to make?"

Urquhart looked at Steph, who looked at Nick and smiled. A catalogue of jazz albums swung open in his head. 'Miles? Perhaps. Benny Goodman or Lionel Hampton? Possibly.' "Err anything by Billie Holiday would be great!" Miss Fernside smiled. "Certainly." She shuffled off enthusiastically in the direction of a polished Steinway on the stage at the far end, opening with *What a little moonlight will do.*

"Why did you refer to the *Normandie* as ill-fated?" Steph asked as their sole course arrived.

"It caught fire in New York harbour in 1941 during a re-fit and sank. The Americans had planned to convert it into a troop ship carrying 15,000 soldiers to Europe – more than seven times its original capacity. In civilian service - when I knew it - there was accommodation for just under 2000 passengers. It was unquestionably the most extravagantly fitted liner that ever sailed. What many believe 'jinxed' the project was that the Americans intended to 're-launch' her as *USS Lafayette*."

The captain slowly shook his head. "Never a good idea renaming a ship."

"So where is she now – the wreck of the *Normandie / Lafayette*?" Nick asked.

"In a ship breakers' yard in New Jersey."

"And all those Lalique mirrors?" Steph wondered.

Urquhart gave a wry smile. "I shouldn't think they ever left New York."

It was when their waiter was removing their soup bowls that the puzzled chaperone asked the skipper: "This morning we saw you fling that marker buoy to guide the rescuers in the lifeboat. How on earth did you know where to place it?"

"Well, I knew from the sound the moment I switched the ship's power to 'idle' after that first 'Man Overboard' cry and I knew from monitors on the bridge what turbulence we were encountering. I added the two distances together – and just threw as hard as I could."

"Judging by that young rating's tragic discovery," Stephenie observed, "your calculations were spot on."

Urquhart gave a gracious nod of thanks as Nick slid the embossed menu card to his left. "May I make a small request, Captain?"

"Ask away, young man."

"Would you be kind enough to sign this for me? I should like to send it to my mother in England." The captain took a pen from his jacket and signed a corner with a flourish.

Dinner was over by 10 o'clock and Steph was all for hitting the sack. They took their leave of the skipper at the entrance to the Dining Room, giving a wave of thanks to Miss Fernside as she gamely ploughed through the Billie Holiday songbook.

"There's something I need to look up in the Library," Nick told the chaperone. "So, I'll say 'goodnight'. See you in the morning."

He made his way along a deserted companionway, intending to write a short message to his mother on the menu card, which he would post in the Purser's office on his way to breakfast. Up ahead, he spotted two young stewards wearing what appeared to be fancy dress costumes.

Both were 'blacked up' and wore frizzy golliwog wigs and carried red party balloons. And most unusually, both were wearing their uniforms – mess jackets and trousers - inside out. After rapping on several cabin doors they disappeared around a corner giggling.

At breakfast Stephenie carefully took her charges through the questions of her quiz, which they had all morning to complete. Brainy Stephen wanted to know how they were expected to discover which was Charles Dickens' longest novel ("go to the ship's Library and find the book with the most pages", Nick suggested helpfully).

And Annie didn't understand the question: 'Name the famous film actress whose name starts with 'Z', who can be seen in a photo on the wall in the Gift Shop, surrounded by hat boxes.'

"Come with me after breakfast and I'll show you the picture," Stephenie reassured the girl. "Oh and guess what: there's a special film treat for you all tonight: *Robin Hood, Prince of Thieves*. I can promise you it has the best sword fight ever filmed!"

A young steward appeared at the chaperone's side, offering her a small envelope on a silver tray.

"Captain's compliments, ma'am."

'Thank you for your company last night', the card read. *I have a small knotty problem which I need to resolve. Could you join me on The Bridge at 10.00 hrs and I will explain all. Yours T.'*

Stephenie consulted her watch: 9.45. "I'll be back before lunchtime if there are any more queries. Or else ask Nick or Stephen." After escorting Annie to the Gift Shop and 'introducing' her to the picture of Zsa Zsa Gabor, she followed the young steward down a companionway until they reached a small white doorway marked THE BRIDGE. CREW ONLY.

Inside the doorway was a flight of steps almost as steep as a ladder, at the top of which was a matching door with a KNOCK BEFORE ENTERING sign set beneath its circular observation window.

Steph knocked and nervously entered this Holy of Holies.
 The Bridge was as broad as the ship itself, dominated by a curved line of raked square windows looking out to sea. At each end of this glazed panorama was an angled window, set at 90 degrees, beneath which was a matching 'glass floor' of wired glass to give views of the harbourside when docking. The floor was in narrow strips of bleached oak, with an ebony border.

Centre stage, set behind a formidable array of nautical hardware and elevated on a chrome pedestal was the Captain's seat, upholstered in white leather with dark blue piping. It was presently unoccupied. Urquhart's Second Officer, a slim young woman of about 35 stood studying a bronze-coloured glass orb.

She turned on hearing Steph knock and enter. "Good morning, ma'am. Welcome to The Bridge. I'm Brenda. The Skipper will be right with you." She gestured to a small table in the corner, on which there was a jug of coffee and two cups.

Stephenie had barely taken her seat when Tom Urquhart appeared, with a large pair of Zeiss binoculars slung around his neck. "I hope you and young Nicholas enjoyed last night," he began.

"We most certainly did. I can't thank you enough. Nicholas was especially impressed by Miss Fernside's Billie Holiday repertoire."

Urquhart leaned back in his chair and gave a gracious smile. "A real 'find' isn't she? Comes on all our trips. Look, I'd value your advice, Stephenie – if I may call you that?"

"Of course."

"We're due to reach the Meridian in just over five hours. Which means, of course, that we shall be 'Crossing the Line' – an ancient nautical tradition which all vessels rigorously observe."

He fingered the handle of his coffee cup thoughtfully. "I took soundings amongst my officers over breakfast and all agreed it should go ahead. But in view of yesterday's tragedy, I'm rather loathe to make our ceremony too flamboyant. Just a simple half-hour celebration, perhaps?"

"I'm a bit 'at sea' here, so to speak" Stephenie told him. "Are these events normally very colourful?"

"Can be. P&O have quite a reputation in that department. Some go on into the night!"

"How many would be involved?"

The skipper pulled a blue notebook from his jacket pocket and flipped it open. "Well, to start with there's me: King Neptune. I'm normally attended by two mermaids. There are two girls in the Laundry who always fill that bill admirably. Then there's Davey Jones. He doesn't normally have to speak, but what with yesterday, references to his Locker would hardly be a good idea. Miss Fernside will provide the musical accompaniment on her accordion. Which leaves only you."

"Me?"

"Would you do me the honour of being the Sea Goddess Amphitrite? You don't have a speaking part – but we'll have to fit you out in a goddess-like costume." He gave a smile. "The laundry girls will be good at that."

"I'd be… honoured, Tom. Petrified but honoured!"

He flipped his notebook shut. "Good, that's settled. Rendezvous in front of the pool on the top deck at 14.30 hrs. Wear that blue number you had on last night." Urquhart – though charm himself - had reverted to 'full Captain Mode'.

A small area between the fo'c's'le and the pool had been cordoned off with blue ropes. There was the Gym Manager, disguised as Davey Jones in a black frock coat, thigh-length boots and a huge tricorn hat (though not carrying his traditional leather-bound ledger marked DAVEY JONES' LOCKER).

The girls from the Laundry (armed with a hamper of nautical accessories) were already in place when Neptune arrived, carrying his trident and wearing a floor-length silver cloak, borne by the same two Polliwogs Nick had spotted the previous evening.

The giggling laundry girls had soon festooned Steph's hair with artificial seaweed, capping the additions with a mitre-shaped 'crown' made from pieces of coral.

Just before the appointed hour Miss Fernside arrived, carrying an impressive red Italian Soprani accordion, slung from one shoulder by an embroidered strap. She wore a red tam o' shanter, a cream silk blouse over an olive green kilt and a pair of salmon pink lace-up boots. Unclipping the accordion, she drew air into the bellows, stamped the deck three times and set a hot opening pace with *Hooray and up she rises.*

At the appointed hour Neptune banged his trident on the deck for silence. "When the ship's horn sounds, My Hearties, I want you to give three rousing cheers as we Cross the Line. Then please join us for a Nautical Tea in the Ballroom."

Perth Horizon gave an impressively long blast on its steam horn at precisely 15.00 hrs and passengers' cameras were soon produced to photograph the performers as Miss Fernside broke into a nautical medley.

After dutifully posing for the cameras for the best part of quarter-on-an-hour Amphitrite moved around the fo'c's'le's railings. Nick followed her lead until they were standing side-by-side, silently surveying the gentle furrow the ship's prow was making. Steph removed her precious coral crown, nudged Nick's elbow and gestured to a disturbance on the sea's surface off the starboard bow.

Two mature dolphins were 'accompanying' the ship, playfully arcing and dipping through the waves.

Suddenly, ahead of the pair a much younger dolphin, with lighter markings, appeared. Many of the ship's passengers had now spotted this unusual phenomenon and were furiously snapping away.

Nick took Steph's arm gently. "Let's go and join Neptune's tea party, shall we?" Steph momentarily held back for one final look at the dolphins' display.

As they descended the staircase leading to the Ballroom, Stephenie clasped Nick's hand and whispered: "I think the young one in front was Ian."

The spread which greeted them surpassed all the Galley's previous creations. The table centrepiece was a most convincing chocolate blancmange miniature of Neptune clasping a silver icing sugar trident, in the centre of a huge oval dish, surrounded by a 'sea' of small dates cut as fish shapes, edged by samphire. There were scallop-shaped egg sandwiches and a platter of sardines on toast.

* * *

After an early evening of Bingo (only the older ones like brainy Stephen had bothered to stay up) Nick decided to turn in and wished Steph good night. "I'll be giving the results of my quiz after breakfast in the morning," she told him. On his way to his cabin Nick asked a steward at what hour they would be in Cape Town. "We're due to dock at 6.45 am. Not many passengers leaving, sir."

"There's one I particularly want to say 'goodbye' to. Could you give me a call at 6.15 am?"

"Certainly sir."

Much as he would like to have witnessed Errol Flynn and Basil Rathbone duelling, Nick had had enough excitement for one day.

* * *

Dressed in his grey cotton gym track suit, Nick stood by the gang plank on A Deck as *Perth Horizon* gently navigated its way along the approaches to Cape Town harbour. There was an early-morning chill in the air and no other passengers on deck.

"Fancy a grog, sir?" Standing beside him was one of the Polliwogs, his steward's uniform now worn the correct way around.

"What's 'a grog'?"

"Brandy, hot water, cinnamon and a fresh slice of lemon," came the enthusiastic reply.

"OK, I'll give it a try." The young steward rushed off with the order.

Nick felt the ship cautiously nudge against the jetty just as Col Newman appeared, carrying a briefcase. He was again wearing his grey hound's tooth suit and Commando tie. This morning, he was also sporting a Commando beret as head gear.

"I say, young man, you're up devilishly early, aren't you?"

"I just wanted to wish you lots of luck at the reparation conference."

"Why, thank you. I think I'll need it." He let the steward walk ahead with his luggage on a trolley and felt in his jacket pocket, removing a Bryant & May match carton, which he rattled. "*And I've got my lucky talisman! Hope you get on ok in Oz; I'm sure you will. Why not drop me a line care of The Bursar at Bancrofts?*" The Colonel threw Nick a smart salute and trudged towards the gang plank.

14

PERTH

THE SHIPPING LANES of Perth, originally fashioned by the first Scottish settlers in the 1850s, were calm and uncluttered at 6.00 am, as Captain Tom Urquhart stood on the Bridge guiding *Perth Horizon* down the Swan River and King George's Sound, moving forwards slowly on a single screw. Ahead, a brace of tugs, hovered like mother hens, awaiting the signal to take over.

The Skipper gave a short blast on his horn, the signal for two deck hands to fling out the ship's tow lines. Under escort, *Perth Horizon* edged closer to landfall in Western Australia and the completion of her 10,000-mile voyage.

Nick Jones, dressed in a track suit and perched on the fo'c's'le was the only passenger up at this hour. Down at dock level the only sign of activity was the arrival of a huge blue Fordson flat-bedded lorry, which the driver parked at the jettyside.

Four figures emerged from a cabin and hailed him. One of the men broke away from the group and began to ascend a long vertical steel ladder fixed to the tallest of the dockside derricks. He climbed into its cab and started its engine, simultaneously lowering its lifting hooks, watched by two stevedores and the banksman. The long jib swung out over the ship.

Aboard the liner, two young deck hands were removing the tarpaulin covering of a huge box-like item of cargo which had been on the aft deck – in all weathers – since Tilbury. Beneath its weatherproof covering was a giant whitewood packing case, twice as high as a saloon car, with the Ford motor company's logo stamped on its side. One of the deck hands was now on top of the boxwood crate, fixing the crane's hooks into steel lifting rings. Both deck hands stood back as the crane driver's banksman gave him the traditional 'take the strain' signal of a clutched fist. The loose chains tightened and the crate was slowly eased from the deck. Hardwood packing 'baulks' were slid from under the box and thrown down onto the dockside to be placed on the flatbed of the lorry by the driver.

The man in the derrick's cab was clearly an expert at safely guiding weighty cargo from ship to shore, as without drama the mighty Ford packing case settled – like a tired dog into its basket – onto the baulks lined up on the bed of the lorry. The lorry's leaf springs and tyres sagged in response. Grinning, the stevedores shook hands with the banksman and the two deckhands who had joined them.

Nick saw the group of seven being joined by a distinguished figure in sparkling white, carrying a satchel on his shoulder. Captain Urquhart, who had come down from the Bridge to add his thanks, produced a Polaroid camera from the bag, formed the group up behind the lorry's tailgate and took their photo. They were clearly amazed at the 'instant' print it produced. A second shot was taken for the shipping line's files and the gathering broke up with much jovial back-slapping.

As they all tailed away, Nick watched the lorry driver affixing a promotional banner to the back of the huge packing case. It read FORDSON COMBINE HARVESTER. Underneath (as if adding an insulting footnote for Nick's benefit): were the words DAGENHAM UK.

Watching the huge white crate being hauled out of the docks, Nick recalled the brief moment in Wanstead when he'd watched a Plessey lorry reverse out of the station yard, with a load marked 'A-P D x 8'. Which, given all the nudge-nudging that went on in The George, certainly weren't Christmas decorations. 144 per shift the chargehand had more than once boasted. Anti-Personnel Devices! Now wouldn't that be a conversational googly to bowl in the dorm at Forest? "I briefly had a torrid affair in the summer holidays with an older woman – until I discovered she worked in an underground munitions factory."

At 7.00 am the Ballroom was abuzz with chatter about their early-morning arrival. Stephenie valiantly waded through to the tail end of her quiz. The ginger twins had done well, but poor Annie just couldn't get her head around how to pronounce Zsa

Zsa Gabor's name. "Say it like 'Shah'" suggested the Sea Goddess.

"'Shah?' What's that?"

"He's the King of Persia. Right, so who's got 12 out of 12? No-one. 11? 10?" One of the ginger twins raised Stephen's arm. "Well done, Stephen. Right, here's your gift voucher. Cut along to the Gift Shop and get something nice for your mother. I'll post it to her for you when I get back to England." As he went to leave (with his two ginger-headed escorts) Steph asked him: "How on earth did you find the answer to the question: 'Name the nearest township to Hollow Tree Farm'?"

As if addressing a 6-year-old, the boy replied: "I looked at the label on my cabin trunk."

A smiling Captain Urquhart had joined the group, clearly relieved that the combine harvester had been successfully 'landed' and was now on its way across Western Australia. "So, has your chaperone briefed you about Perth's Immigration?" he asked Nick, placing a fatherly hand on his shoulder.

"Not really. Why, is there a problem?"

"Not so long as all your travel documents and certificates of immunisation are in order. But tread very carefully, my boy: The Immigration Officers here are tough cookies. Always answer their questions politely. If it's a man, say 'Sir'; if it's a woman address her as 'Ma'am.'"

"Understood." Just like Forest School, Nick thought to himself.

The skipper lowered his voice to a conspiratorial whisper. "Behind the officers' desks is a frosted glass door marked PORT OFFICE. That connects with the large bus pick-up point for all transfers. The only control for that door is a button on the floor, operated by the immigration officers, which releases a catch. Until you hear *that* catch click and pass though *that* doorway you haven't entered Australia." He patted the boy on the back. "The very best of luck, Nicholas!"

At the head of the gangplank leading down to the dockside, Nick paused to reflect on Urquhart's warning. At this hour he could certainly do without the sort of 'going over' he'd received so many times from Forest School's prefects.

One of the Polliwogs cheerily waved up to him, standing guard over his black cabin trunk. He gave the youth the 'thumbs up' and slung his canvas fisherman's satchel over his shoulder.

"Where to boss?"

"There's supposed to be a green-and-cream single-decker bus waiting in the yard the other side of the Immigration Office. It should say 'Hollow Tree Farm'. He handed the youth a folded $5 note.

The long cavernous Immigration Hall was hot and stuffy and poorly-lit by unmasked neon tubes.

Four parallel rows of unupholstered pine benches – already three-quarters full – faced across the remaining space to a trio of desks, each manned by a uniformed immigration officer. There were two middle-aged men, with a stern-looking grey-haired woman between them.

Behind the officials hung the inevitable photo-portraits of King George VI, Queen Elizabeth and Field-Marshall Slim of Burma. The walls behind the waiting area displayed aerial photographs of Sydney Harbour Bridge, the Great Barrier Reef and King George's Sound, which *Perth Horizon* had navigated that morning.

'Hamilton!' barked the pa system, as a buzzing noise simultaneously clicked open the Hall's Exit door, momentarily allowing shafts of sunshine and fresh air to enter. A young woman slipped out. The Port Office's door slammed shut as Mr Hamilton nervously approached the vacated desk.

'How on earth can this miserable-looking trio of pen-pushers handle a mob of at least 30 weary travellers?' Nick mused to himself. Alphabetically, he might be in with a shout he thought.

"Johnson?" Click, bang. Mr Hamilton was outside in a flash, like a greyhound from a trap.

The grey-haired matron tidied the papers on her desktop, realigned a collection of pens and pencils and straightened the formidable 'armoury' of brass hand-franking stamps. "Jones!" the tannoy barked. Nick slung his shoulder bag up and approached the desk. Silently she turned the pages of his application. His cheery 'Good morning' failed to elicit any reaction. He wouldn't have been surprised if her first words had been: "And when did you last see your father?" He took a seat.

Slowly she worked her way through the pages without looking up at the applicant once. Finally, she asked: "And what is the nature of your visit?"

'Hmmm – an easy one to start' the batsman thought. 'Just play it straight back to the bowler.

"I have been accepted as a pupil at the residential farm school of Hollow Tree Farm, near Malvern Creek, Western Australia, Ma'am."

"Duration?"

"Unspecified. To the best of my knowledge." Another blocking stroke. They had yet to make eye contact. The officer decided to change tactics, using a longer run-up. She paused to scratch a new starting point in the turf with her studded boot and moved the ball around in her curled fist, so that it's yellow stitching appeared between her two middle fingers.

"And you arrived on the *SS Perth Horizon* this morning. How many in your party?"

He blocked this one and waited until it was a 'dead ball', before flicking it to a slip fielder.

"Initially there was 28 of us, Ma'am."

"Initially?"

"One of our party was lost at sea, Ma'am." It grieved Nick to say the words.

The end of the over. He'd survived.

The Matron looked up for the first time to slowly study Nick's tear-filled eyes. She fitted the top to her fountain pen and laid it on its stand, lifted Nick's application documents and tapped them on end into a tidy bundle. As she placed them in a tray marked OUT a large mechanical clanking noise came from beneath the desk and the door of the Port Office swung open. "You may go."

15

HINDSIGHT

MARGARET AND JOHN Gray were Mimi's oldest friends in the Eagle Court community. It was Dr Gray who had taken Mimi and Nick to Tilbury Docks for Nick's leave-taking for Australia.

A fortnight after that sad journey Mimi rang Margaret Gray. "I was wondering if I could pop over to discuss a quasi-medical problem with John, even though he's not my GP. Frankly, Margaret, I find talking to Henry O'Toole is like talking to a brick wall."

"Of course you can dear. John won't be in late tonight, so come over at about 7.30; we'll have had our supper."

The Grays lived in a ground floor apartment similar in layout to Mimi's, but closer to the railway line. The VII blast had only shattered one window in their kitchen. Their two sons, John – a near contemporary of Nick – and younger Richard were both at boarding school.

Mimi settled herself on the sofa and told Margaret Gray: "I'd quite like it if you'd sit in too. I'd value another woman's opinion."

Avuncular John Gray entered and took the armchair opposite. "So, what's troubling you, Mimi?"

Mimi gazed at the clutch bag in her lap, suddenly tongue-tied for words. "It's Nick."

"Yes, I'd guessed as much. Must be very hard living alone, when both of the men you've shared your life with have gone." Mimi nodded but made no reply.

"Sleeping ok?" She shook her head.

"Getting out and about?" Again, she shook her head.

"Not even to Grandma Jones at Rozel?"

She shrugged. "Once a week, with her order from the butchers. I don't think she's noticed, but I don't go round there so often. These days she seems to be wholly engrossed in her horse racing."

"Well, I can give you a mild sedative to help you catch up on some of that missing sleep. But that's not the root cause of it all, Mimi, is it?" She shook her head.

"My dear old mother in Kirkcaldy often used to chide me, when I was a medical student and struggling with revision for exams: 'Don't be a What-iffer, John.' You know hindsight's a wonderful thing, Mimi."

"I couldn't agree more, John. But endless late-night reflections make me realise what a *fait accompli* I handed my son. And the information – such as it was – from that Australia House official took him less than 20 minutes to impart!"

Margaret Gray intervened. "How long must Nick stay on at this farm school place?"

"Two years. Then it's up to him to fend for himself. Most probably he'll finish up as no more than an hourly-paid farm labourer."

"Unless he can raise the money for a passage back home?" Mimi nodded.

"Have you thought about going down there to rescue him?" John Gray suddenly enquired. She was shocked by the directness of his enquiry.

"All the time! What d'you think it is keeps me awake half the night, John?"

"And Denise – your co-organiser? What's her opinion?"

Mimi brightened up for the first time since the discussion started. "I've not said a word to my sister. Visiting Australia House and being interviewed by that reptile Mr J J Codrington, was not the smartest of moves, though it all seemed like a good idea at the time." The Grays stared at each other, shocked by the uncharacteristic ferocity of Mimi's outburst.

After a long pause Dr John Gray told Mimi: "If you did decide to go down to Perth, Mimi – at your own expense - with a view to removing your son from this farm school arrangement before the completion of his two-year placement – it's more than likely that either the Australian or the British government would send you a bill."

"For what, exactly?" Mimi snapped.

"For breaking the terms of their Assisted Passages programme."

"I think John's right, Mimi," Margaret Gray confirmed.

Mimi Jones gave a wan smile. "I think I'd rather cross that bridge when I come to it!"

The Scottish doctor, surmising that Mimi had probably taken all she could manage (and none of it exactly encouraging) nodded to his wife to rustle up some coffees. He reached into his waistcoat pocket and fished out a small pad, to write her a prescription for the sedatives.

* * *

The following morning Mimi rang the London office of the Cunard shipping line and asked to be put through to general enquiries about passenger travel to Australia.

"When exactly was madam hoping to travel?" a male clerk enquired.

"I'm fairly flexible. Would the departure point be Tilbury?"

"Southampton, madam. Just one person travelling?"

"Yes."

"First or second class?"

"Second."

"Port of arrival?"

"It must be Perth."

After a long pause (and the sound of much paper shuffling) the booking clerk came back on the line. "This is slightly out-of-the-ordinary, madam, but in 10 days' time our *SS Lord Nelson* will be departing Southampton for Perth, calling only at Gibraltar."

"How is that unusual?"

"Because only 50 per cent of the vessel will be available for passengers – cabins, restaurants and so forth. The forward half of the vessel is being re-fitted as it was requisitioned during the last war as a troop carrier. The half of the ship you'd be using is brand new."

"Can you give me an all-inclusive price for a cabin?"

"I've got a nice single berth on B Deck, portside, which I can offer you for £120; payment within seven days of written confirmation. You'll not be troubled by the refurbishment works I can assure you."

There was a long silence as Mimi desperately tried to remember how much hard currency was actually sitting in the Quality Street tin in the pantry. She paused, cleared her voice and in her best 'cut glass' intonation told the clerk: "Yes, that will be quite acceptable. A cheque will be in the post in the morning if you will kindly give me the address."

She hurried into the kitchen to drag out the Quality Street tin, then methodically 'cashed up' its contents, disregarding IOUs and receipts. There was sufficient to cover the cheque that she would need to get Matt to write for her. And at the very bottom of the various scraps of paper she came across an official receipt from a book dealer in Farringdon Road. It simply said: 'To sale of Builder Group's leather-bound memorial album *The Life & Times of Isambard Kingdom Brunel* (with six steel engravings by Evans Bros): £120.' A quick trip 'Down Under', funded by Alan's Brunel volume, seemed highly appropriate.

* * *

"Henshaw residence."

"Marion? It's Mimi Jones. Sorry to trouble you, but could I have a quick word with Matthew if he's returned from work?"

"Certainly, dear. I'll call him."

"Matt here, Mrs Jones."

"I've a small favour to ask you, dear. It concerns the 'Quality Street Fund'".

"Ask away."

"Well, tomorrow I need to post a cheque for a payment. And as Nicholas will doubtless have told you, I am considered *persona non grata* as far as Wanstead's banks are concerned. So, I was wondering, Matthew, if I was to – so to speak – cover the amount in cash from the Quality Street Fund - whether you would be willing to give me a cheque for the equivalent?"

"Sure. How shall I get it to you; by post?"

"Is there any way you could bring it to Eagle Court tomorrow?"

"Let's see - well on Thursdays I always have a tutorial with one of the partners. In the office. They never start before 10.30 am; so 'yes' I could drop it into Eagle Court, then catch the Underground at Snaresbrook."

"Perfect."

"So, what's the amount?"

"£120."

"Right you are. Payable to?"

"Cunard Lines."

After a long pause, Matthew Henshaw asked: "So which exotic location are you sailing off to with Cunard, Mrs Jones — the Caribbean?"

"Australia!" she cried enthusiastically, feeling happy for the first time.

16

PAPER TRAIL

FLUSHED WITH HER success at securing a heavily-discounted passage to Australia, Mimi had a light breakfast of toast and marmalade. Matt's cheque lay in front of her on the kitchen table; all she had to do was get it in the mid-day post to Cunard's head office. Matt had left his bike in the garage, saying he would call for it after 6.00 pm and then cycle home to Chigwell.

It was the fine detail of Mimi's headstrong decision to go down to Western Australia to rescue her son which was now beginning to trouble her. What would be her 'cover story' for the ever-vigilant Mr Parker, Eagle Court's caretaker? Or her next-door neighbours, the elderly Derbyshires? Should she let Denise in on the plot? And what possible excuse could she give for her sudden disappearance to her mother-in-law, the aged but sharp-as-a-pin Nana Belle, who, rather surprisingly hadn't yet commented on the absence of her gambling partner.

After finishing her toast, she ventured into Nick's bedroom. On a bookshelf, between his stamp album and collection of Tour de Fance press cuttings, she located what she was looking for: a postcard album – plastic sleeves containing souvenir messages from members of the family - from British seaside spas to exotic scenes of palm-fringed beaches in Ceylon. Most carried long hand-written messages; but a few (which Nick had probably purchased in seaside souvenir shops) were blank. It was the blanks that she sought.

A painstaking trawl of the album netted just three: a snow-capped Ben Nevis; her brother-in-law Guy ascending the famous Shelsey Walsh hill climb in an ERA; and a tree-lined avenue in the National Trust's beautiful Hidcote Gardens in Gloucestershire.

* * *

Matthew's timing was perfect. "Get that cheque off in the post ok?" he asked.

"It's on its way. Now we need to discuss Phase 2 of my Master Plan." She poured him some tea.

"Oh yes, and what might that be?"

"Why, my 'cover story - for my mysterious Agatha Chrisie-like disappearance. I might be able to pull the wool over the neighbours' eyes with some cock-and-bull story about visiting my sister in Chipping Camden, but there's not much that slips past Nana Belle, you know?"

Matthew rocked back on the kitchen chair and nodded. "I can believe that!"

Without explanation, she laid out the three 'blank' postcards she'd taken from her son's collection, akin to a card sharp tantalisingly laying down playing cards for the three-card trick. 'Click. Click. Click.'

"So what's this: 'Guess the name of the famous tourist attraction'?"

"Sort of. But with a subtle nuance, Matthew. I'm planning to lay down an elaborate 'paper trail' (she stabbed at the trio of postcard views) – Scotland, Worcestershire, Gloucestershire - charting my imaginary travels around the British Isles, while in reality I'll be on my way to Australia."

"Who will they be sent to?"

"All to Nana Belle at Rozel. Written and signed by me. Posted first from Edinburgh, to be followed by a second message to her from me, allegedly in Bromyard, Herefordshire. And finally, one from my sister Juliette in Gloucestershire. We often visit Hidcote when I stay down there."

"Who posts them?"

"That's where I'm hoping your fiancée can help. If I was to write, address and stamp them, would she be willing to drop them in a letterbox at set intervals - or get a friend in Scotland? We'll just have to take pot luck that Nana Belle doesn't spot the Leytonstone postmarks on the other two."

"Sounds OK."

"The timing will be crucial, Matt. If Moira despatches them at, say, three-week intervals, it should just give me time to get back from Perth."

As with the pricing of re-conditioned golf balls, young Matthew couldn't be easily bamboozled into something. He stroked his chin and looked at the view of Ben Nevis. "Mmm. Might work."

"Might work? MIGHT work! It's jolly well got to work! Or else Nicholas and I will be the social pariahs of Wanstead! And by the way: the caretaker here Mr Parker is to be fed the same Tour of England line."

Matt looked at his watch. "Listen, I must make tracks. If Mum rings, say I'm on my way. D'you think I could I borrow one of Nick's cycle lamps?"

She pulled a key from a hook under the draining board. Help yourself. You won't recognise our garage – it looks more like a cycle accessories shop. Ask Moira to ring me in the morning, would you, dear?"

* * *

"So how can I help?" Moira asked the next day. "Matthew says you want me to post some cards for you while you're away."

"Yes please. They will be pre-written and stamped tourist postcards – all to be sent to Nana Belle."

"Shouldn't be a problem. Matt said there would be three."

"That's it. One – allegedly – from Edinburgh, one from Herefordshire and one from Gloucestershire. I could send them to you as a package in one large envelope, if you give me your address."

"At three-week intervals, he said."

"Yes, that's the whole idea behind my little ruse, you see: to lay down a sort of Paper Trail across Britain, giving the impression that Nick and I are away sight-seeing, before he starts at college. When in fact - with any luck - we'll be on our way home from Australia! I'll number the envelopes for you in pencil."

Having absorbed the details, Moira's enthusiastic response was: "Mimi – how most ingenious you are! It's a bit like homing pigeons, isn't it?"

"Sorry, dear, I don't follow."

"A very English and Scottish working class sport, you know? In the north of England breeders of racing pigeons take their prize birds, put them in small cages and take them to a railway station, where they are put in the guard's van. At the train's destination – say, Birmingham – the guard releases the pigeon, which instinctively knows how to navigate its way home, back to its pigeon loft!"

"So the three postcards will be my pigeons?"

"Exactly! And Rozel will be their pigeon loft."

* * *

Mimi made herself a mug of Ovaltine to take into the bedroom. The logistics of her ingenious 'paper trail' had exhausted her, though she was heartened by the positive reaction of both Moira and Matt. Tomorrow she would set about composing three postcard messages to her mother-in-law.

In the bedroom she turned on Alan's old HMV radio, expecting to hear the Home Service news bulletin and Shipping Forecast. The announcer was Alvar Liddel, a regular client at Maurice's hairdressing salon in Bond Street.

'Today is the fourth anniversary of the tragic death of that remarkable Mozambique-born vocalist and musician Al Bowlly, cruelly struck down by a German parachute mine at his apartment in St James after returning from an engagement in Buckinghamshire. He was only 43 and some popular music critics said, at the time of his passing, that he could easily have become as famous as Bing Crosby." Before the chimes of Big Ben, the mellifluous strains of the opening riff of Bowlly's best-known ballad filled Mimi's bedroom.

Love is the sweetest thing, what else on earth could ever bring
Such happiness to everything, as love's old story.
Love is the strangest thing, no song of birds upon the wing
Shall in our hearts more sweetly sing than love's old story.

17

HOLLOW TREE FARM

FROM THE AIR the panoramic view a Harrier would get – floating languidly on a thermal in search of its next meal – was that the layout of Hollow Tree Farm was isolated but compact.

"Ten minutes to go folks," the bus driver called. The children eagerly scanned the bleak horizon for their destination, though in the last 15 miles the landscape had changed only marginally, with no signs of perimeter boundaries, until eventually some rather primitive post-and-wire fencing appeared (the posts being sawn lengths of old telegraph poles linked together by rusty barbed wire).

Approached by an unmetalled road from the west, and with the neighbouring township of Malvern Creek shimmering in the distance to the east, there was precious little else to see. Vegetation was sparse and the only sign of life was a small cluster of merino sheep valiantly attempting to gain shelter beneath an ancient laurel tree, which hung over the rusted corrugated roof of a lop-sided out-building. Parked in front of this shed was a grey Ferguson tractor.

Hollow Tree Farm's most dominant building – fashioned in a quasi-Colonial style – was long, two stories high and with a grandiose open veranda extending its full width, furnished with striped armchairs and cushions. Hanging from one of the veranda's rafters was a huge triangular-shaped steel 'gong' which appeared to have been fashioned from a section of disused railway track. This was the official residence of the farm school's Principal, Brigadier Giles Perbright and his wife Glynis.

To one side of the main building was a kitchen wing (judging by the collection of zinc waste containers strewn outside), while on the other flank was the school's timber-clad assembly hall: an uninspiring imitation of a cross between an English public library and a Methodist chapel. It too was in need of a lick of paint.

Facing the long incongruous Raj-like edifice was a diamond-shaped Rounders pitch, not grassed but with a raked sand top. Sheltering the 'diamond' and looking towards the two-storied building was a shallow arc of the single-storied cabins which housed the farm school's children. All had flaking brown-stained weather-boarded sides and felt roofs. In several places, where strong winds had lifted the roofs' covering, they had been 'patched' with rusty corrugated metal sheeting, giving them an unattractive 'piebald' appearance. To a passing tourist bus (or the Harrier for that matter), the somewhat peripatetic nature of Hollow Tree Farm's building maintenance programme was all too evident. The pristine condition of the Principal's Residence was a glaring exception.

The children's cabins' poorly-painted window frames had neither curtains nor mosquito netting. Above the entrance of each cabin was a metal-framed hanging sign identifying each building: Alamy, Dingo, Fringe Valley Orchid, Kangaroo, Kalbarri, Koala, Kunzea and Mula Mula. Bedsheets hung from the front rails of two of the cabins. The farm school's compliment – staff and pupils – hovered around 40.

The Perth Harbour transfer bus came to a halt. The driver had done this trip enough times to know that this was certainly not these poor immigrant children's 'Eureka Moment'.

They cautiously stepped down into the evening heat. Nick whispered to Stephenie: "So is this your second visit?"

"No, my first, actually. Last time Blue Line wanted a swift turn-round, so I never got to see Hollow Tree Farm."

Still no adult staff had appeared from the buildings. The driver began unloading all the children's luggage onto two hand carts. Though the new arrivals were anxious to explore their quaint timber cabins, Stephenie was more preoccupied by a swarthy figure, standing in the shadows of the mansion's veranda, studying them through binoculars. Then, seeing two figures approaching the bus, she whispered to Nick: "Ah ha – I think this could be the Reception Committee!" It was a tall, sun-tanned youth in jeans, holding the hand of a petite blonde-haired girl half his age. She wore a red pleated tartan skirt and a white blouse and was carrying a business-like clip board.

"Welcome you-all to Hollow Tree Farm," the youth said with a big smile and a strong antipodean accent.

Eight-year-old Betty from Birmingham was the most able and experienced of Mrs Perbright's (unpaid) kitchen staff. Orphaned Betty was a veritable powerhouse of efficiency and dexterity. Her dawn-to-dusk duties included: delivering the Brigadier's cooked breakfast to his office; serving all resident House Mothers in the Assembly Hall; supervising washing up; and running haberdashery errands to and from Malvern for Mrs Perbright. The Brigadier's wife (nominally in charge of all the farm school's catering) rarely appeared in public, unless for the reception of dignitaries, such as local councillors or school inspectors. Betty's father had been a Birmingham master butcher killed at Arnhem, who had vouchsafed to her the secrets of making pork sausages with herbs, apples and onions: always the culinary high point of Hollow Tree Farm's Anzac Day supper, which followed the annual Rounders competition. Betty's compatriot Lewis was from South Island, New Zealand. He ably took control of the allocation of cabin accommodation and luggage delivery (all watched by the shadowy figure on the balcony), making the newcomers feel welcome.

* * *

Beyond the kitchens complex and north of the farm's lop-sided workshop was an area of neatly-cultivated land, with rows of root vegetables: potatoes, carrots, parsnips. On this particular boiling hot afternoon two figures could be seen slowly walking backwards down parallel rows, ridging the potatoes.

The figure on the left – wearing only bleached denim shorts – was Lewis, the hired New Zealand hand; his companion and newly-arrived 'apprentice' was Nick Jones, wearing a white shirt over blue jeans. Beyond them – at the furthest point on the potato patch – the sleeping figure of an ill-kempt old woman, dressed in what looked like brown sacking, could be seen stretched out on a bench. Lewis and Nick ignored her, completed their ridging exercise and slumped down under the shade of an acacia.

"Fancy a tinny?" the Kiwi asked.

"Too right, mate!"

The more senior boy got up and ambled towards the workshop, returning with two cans of Fosters lager, which he had removed from the farm manager's unattended office.

Un-protected from the sun's searing rays, the scruffy woman rolled over. Known as Clone 2, Nick had already been warned that this was one of the farm school's sternest House Mothers: the notorious Miss Bromyard, whose autocratic regime was administered with the help of a small riding crop, which she always 'wore' on her wrist. Miss Bromyard, like her half-sister Miss Garway, hailed from Killarney where (so school rumour had it) they had been nuns at one of the infamous Magdalene Laundries, until being de-frocked by the Catholic Church. Their reasons for quitting Killarney could only be speculated at: that all those nautical miles between Southern Ireland and Western Australia would expurgate their crimes.

Lewis produced a small plastic tobacco pouch and offered it to his English companion who declined. Lewis shrugged. "Fancy something stronger?"

"Such as?"

He held up a tiny glass phial and gave a grin.

"What is it?"

"Hash oil. From the Lebanon."

"I'd better not. Thanks all the same."

"No worries."

Miss Bromyard rolled over, tipping the contents of her clutch bag onto the ground. She continued to doze. Lewis tip-toed across, laid his rake on the ground beneath the wooden bench and extracted from her fallen bag a pack of cigarettes.

Resuming his place beneath the tree beside Nick, he withdrew the glass phial's cork top, to which a fine piece of wire was secured. He inserted the wire's end (liberally coated with a treacle-like substance) into one of Miss Bromyard's Full Strength Capstan cigarettes and returned the pack to the opened bag lying under her bench.

Their beer cans were empty by the time the old lady came round. Still half-asleep she felt for her clutch bag, eventually locating it in the dirt. Lewis and Nick watched with fascination as she 'lit up' and took a long draw on the doctored cigarette.

The old crone's inhalation of the Lebanese narcotic seemed to coincide with her bleary-eyed recognition of the long brown handle of Lewis' discarded rake. She shrieked wildly, jumped up and tottered off yelling: "SNAKE! SNAKE!"

* * *

Brigadier Giles Perbright, Principal of Hollow Tree Farm, ran a tight ship, with his gruff domineering style subjugating all before him: his timid wife Glynis (prone to migraines), the staff, the pupils and the only paid employee, Farm Manager Ted Butcher (aka The Bludger). The Kiwi Lewis and little Betty were the only two who would stand up to Perbright. His hero – commemorated by a large portrait photo hanging above the stage in the school's assembly hall – was Field Marshall Slim. It was a moot point whether Perbright ever actually served under Slim, though suggestions that the former had survived the notorious Battle of Kohima sounded to the doubting Kiwi to be 'a bit sus'.

'The Brig's Residence', as it was known to the children, had a strong Indo-Colonial feel to it, with its shaded veranda, used for the entertainment of visiting dignitaries. Surviving UK parents of orphans were strongly discouraged from visiting their offspring and all outgoing mail from the children was officially 'censored'. According to Malvern Creek's Roman Catholic Priest Father Andrew, one distressed mother, who had travelled all the way from England (at her own expense) arriving unannounced to visit her child, was unceremoniously hustled off the site after 48 hours.

Spread out before the Brig's Residence, the children's humble single-storey cabins formed a shallow arc which enclosed the Rounders Square, where traditionally a boy pupils v girl pupils competition was held on ANZAC Day each year, followed by the annual ANZAC Supper, prepared by Betty with the help of casual labour brought in for the night. There were interminable speeches from local dignitaries – whose brief 'blinkered' view of the Brigadier's domain (plus a good meal) only saw the plus points of the farm school system.

One major scandal which was hushed up (and never reported to the English charity which oversaw the farm school's management) was that corporal punishment on the site was restricted (by order of Western Australia's child welfare authority) to male pupils, using only the cane. Perbright simply circumvented this diktat by using his cane swagger stick and making the beatings a public spectacle after supper on Saturdays. Discipline was his watchword.

The English newcomer – remembering his days as a new boy at Forest School – was wise enough to keep an ultra-low profile in his first weeks at Hollow Tree Farm. As far as Perbright was concerned, Nick didn't exist. He shadowed Lewis, who soon introduced him to what the Kiwi classed as 'Cruisy Lurks' – manual jobs out on the farm or in the orchards which simulated hard work – but only when viewed from a distance, such as The Bludger's office in the workshop.

The only time when proper labour was brought in was for the annual shearing of Hollow Tree Farm's small herd of merino sheep. At hay making time, the older boys were used for bale humping, with Lewis behind the controls of the trusty Fergie.

* * *

Breakfast had been cleared and the dish washers stacked. Betty sat alone in the kitchens flicking through a notebook. She was joined by the ginger twins Daisy and Marigold and brainy Simon, now an inseparable trio. Nick and Lewis appeared soon after.

"Right folks," Betty began, "as I'm sure you're all aware, its ANZAC Day next Saturday. And The Brig has asked me to take on the catering as he thinks Glynis is going to go down with one of her migraines."

"I had no idea you could predict a migraine attack 48 hours in advance," observed Simon sarcastically.

"Nor me," agreed little Betty. "But the good news is that the Brig forgot to give me the letters of invitation to the local Big Wigs to post in Malvern. So, it's strictly a Farm School only affair this year, folks. 6.00 pm sharp, straight after the Rounders competition."

"And the menu?" queried Nick.

"I'm just working that out now. Catering for…" she looked across at Lewis. "40?"

He nodded. "Max. There's still several male vacancies to be filled."

"Right, well it's going to be my mum's recipe for shepherd's pie with minced lamb (I've hidden the best cuts in the bottom of the freezer trunk) and one veg; followed by cherry and chocolate fool. Only home-made lemonade to drink. What does everyone think?"

"Go for it!" exclaimed Lewis.

Betty grinned with satisfaction. "Right you be, bro. Then the only ingredients we'll have to import are the cherries and a few bars of plain chocolate. I'll pick them up in Malvern tomorrow. Meat and veg are on the premises or outside."

"Daisy and Marigold: if Lewis gets them for you would you mind chopping up some big onions for the shepherd's pie for me? And we'll need to serve a vegetable with it – like diced carrots. Just be careful with our kitchen knives as they're awful sharp." The twins nodded enthusiastically.

"Stephen: do you know how to prepare chopped walnuts?"

"Not really."

"OK – when Lewis goes to get me some nice fat onions, he can collect a handful of walnuts from the tree growing behind The Bludger's workshop. Bash their shells open with a rolling pin then chop the insides up real fine with a small knife. I'll roast them brown in oil and mix 'em in with the blanched carrots. My roasted walnut carrots always give 'em a shock!"

"And the pudding?" Nick asked.

"I'll wash and stone the cherries and you can make us a nice big bowl of dark chocolate. The two go brilliantly together if you blend them overnight."

Nick recalled a similar combination he'd had at dinner one night on the ship. "It's even smoother if it's got alcohol in it."

Betty wrinkled her nose. "Unfortunately, the farm school's pantries don't run to booze." Then with a wicked twinkle in her eye she added: "But I'll see if I can raid the Brig's cocktail cabinet when I'm dusting later this morning."

* * *

Everyone turned out in their best sporting gear for the annual ANZAC Rounders Tournament.

The previous evening Betty and Lewis had held an hour of voluntary batting practice for the newcomers to familiarise themselves with the game's arcane rules and techniques.

Two things which made Hollow Tree Farm's version of the traditional English ball game unique was that instead of turf it was played on a sand 'diamond' (akin to American baseball) making run-outs far more spectacular. And that a very tempting line of dense brambles, so thick that even the sheep didn't venture into it, immediately behind the pitcher's arm made for some impressive long hits and - much to the Brigadier's annoyance - the loss of another valuable rounders ball. For this year's match, Lewis and Betty had come up with the tempting prize of 4 cans of The Bludger's Fosters lager for the first batter to break a window in the Brig's Residence.

The boys were coasting to a comfortable win in the second innings when Perbright – quite out of character – began favouring the girls with some extremely odd interpretations of the rules. Side arm deliveries were permitted (provided they weren't 'bodyline') but he ruled two as 'no balls' awarding a half-run penalty.

Nick stood stationery at the plate a la Dennis Compton, facing Betty, who sent down an evil spinning delivery which positively curved in mid-air, causing him to side-step half a pace to make better contact. When bat met ball there was a resounding click and it set off in a high arcing trajectory towards the Brigadier's veranda. Forest School's cricket coach Mr Deaton would have dismissed it as 'a cow shot', without finesse. Nevertheless, it made it to the famous triangular gong and its 'musical ricochet' seemed to give the ball extra propulsion. It crashed through one of the office windows, breaking four panes of glass. There were jubilant cheers all round, save for the crestfallen umpire, who pulled off his Ghurkha hat and flung it down into the sand.

* * *

When the blue taxi pulled up by the farm gates, Betty and Stephen were sitting forlornly on a log. Lewis jumped out of the Ford Pilot with mock-enthusiasm, dumping his purchases down on the ground. "Right, all good?" he enquired cheerily.

The boy and the little girl brightened up a little and the trio trooped off towards the Bludger's workshop.

"First off: we've got to create five secure shearing pens," Lewis announced.

"From what, exactly?" queried Stephen.

"Anything we can lay our hands on, mate!"

Ingenuity was the team's watchword and within an hour, five very sturdy shearing pens, formed from spare steel mattress frames from the cabins, supported by fencing posts – two set on one side and the other three separated by a central 'aisle' – had been built down the workshop's central 'spine', leading to the opened double doors to the fenced yard.

Lewis pointed at a floor space by the exit. "Stephen: that's where you're going to have your Foot Rot bath. They all have to run through it to get outside with their mates, after they've been sheared. Just keep topping it up with the mix I'll make for you in that 5-gallon plastic container. But before they go through the 'water hazard' Daisy and Marigold will have to attend to any snips to their skins the shearers have made, using cotton wool Dettol dabs. The sting normally makes 'em jump forward – straight into the trough!"

"What happens to the shorn fleeces?" Nick asked.

Pulling a handful of long oak dowels from his bag Lewis explained: "We did this last year and it worked a treat. I've had a steel 'frame' made from scrap angle iron and these dowels all sit on it in a row. But unfastened." He rattled them. There were times, Nick reflected, when his Kiwi friend possessed many of the entrepreneurial skills of Dickens' Artful Dodger.

Nick and Stephen swung a single fleece onto the wooden rollers, fleece side downwards, and Lewis agitated it with a broom handle. "See: all the rubbish that's accumulated in their wool – leaves, bracken, dead bugs, sheep droppings – falls out into a bin or bucket. You'd be amazed how much rubbish those merinos carry around with them for twelve months. Without complaining.

"Then while you lot have supper, Nick and I are going to pack the cleaned fleeces into those three white packing cases standing in the yard; packing 'em down real solid, inside a protective envelope of hessian. In all the big shearing operations it's done pneumatically. At first light - all being well - they'll be on their way by sea to Sheffield in Yorkshire. And that's about it. Any questions?"

"How many fleeces in total?" Stephen asked.

"There should be 400. That's the size of our flock. Miniscule by Oz standards, I know."

"So how many merinos are there across the whole of Australia?" the ever-inquisitive boy asked.

"Guess."

"A million?"

"Higher. Much higher."

"Surely not 10 million?"

"Currently not far short of 30 million. They're said to have come from Andalucia in the 12th century, originally raised by North African Berbers. Whose idea it was to bring them to Australia isn't recorded, but they just love this hot dry climate. Anybody want to guess how many merinos there are in the UK?"

Silence greeted the question. Lewis formed his thumb and forefinger into a 'zero' as Betty appeared in a white apron, bearing a plate of hot sausage rolls.

"I'll be in charge of shear re-sharpening on the carborundum wheel tomorrow. If you have any problems at all, don't forget they're bringing four roustabouts. And they're all well paid!"

Lewis got Stephen to cut some patterns from thin card to stencil onto the sides and top of the whitewood packing cases. "Is Sheffield where they'll finish up?"

"Nope. That's only half-way, bro. There they'll be cleaned again and carded, then spun onto weaving reels before their next journey."

"To where?"

"Milan, Italy. To be woven into ladies' gowns and gentlemen's suits. Our last job tomorrow night will be to leave these three loaded and sealed packing cases by the front gate for the carrier to collect and take 'em to Brockhampton, where they'll be put onto a goods train for Melbourne."

* * *

Promptly at 7.45 the following morning Betty entered the 'Shearing Shed', wearing a long red-and-white striped apron. Together with one of her kitchen helpers she was carrying a huge two-handled paella pan, its contents a veritable work of culinary art.

Arranged around the edge of the pan was a 'sun ray' of 10 equal segments of black field mushrooms, interspersed with grilled plum tomatoes. Between them were 20 rashers of streaky bacon and 10 of Betty's 'signature' pork, herb and diced apple sausages (known at Hollow Tree as 'Betty's churs'), halved and grilled long-ways. Atop all this sat 10 fried eggs, sunny side up, topped by generous sprinklings of golden-brown croutons. A second helper followed behind with an oval platter of buttered toast and Lewis cracked open the contents one of the Bludger's hidden cases of Fosters. Betty and her aides took a bow and left to a round of applause.

Fired up by Betty's gargantuan breakfast spread, the five shearers worked tirelessly through the morning. Between sheep, which sometimes took as little as 4 minutes, the movements of their electric shears were so deft. Some would grab a swig from a water bottle offered by a roustabout, while others favoured tinnies of Fosters. Nick's job was to re-sharpen the shears on a power-driven carborundum wheel which Lewis had clamped to the edge of the manager's desk. Daisy and Marigold quickly developed a technique for their disinfectant treatment as the shorn sheep made a dash for freedom – splashing through Stephen's anti-foot-rot tray to escape.

"I think the lads may finish early, mate," the manager told Lewis, who was taking a breather outside from fleece cleaning. "We've got to be in Brockhampton by 6.00 pm for supper."

"Are they putting you up?"

"No chance! We've got to sleep in the bus; but I've reserved the back seat! Somehow, I doubt that those folk will have organised such a dinkum breakfast as yours. We're all fair chocka. Remember to get Betty to leave a collecting tin out for the lads to tip her, will you? And I might take a group snap for the record with my Brownie."

The cleaned and washed-out paella pan from breakfast – marked 'BETTY'S BONUS' – was duly left on the floor by the door to the workshop, netting the little cook a staggering $55. Before driving off the manager snapped his team, arm-in-arm with Betty and Lewis in front of the bus. The group photo would be on the front page of the *Malvern Mercury* the following week.

After the shearers' bus had pulled away, Nick, Lewis and Stephen eyed the three massive fleece packing cases. Lewis attempted to rock one corner, but it remained steadfast in the sand.

"So how did you move them last year?" Nick asked.

"On the Fergie's trailer. But the fork lift wasn't knackered then."

Stephen eyed one of the fencing post supports to Lewis's make-shift shearing pens. "You could always roll them. The Egyptians used that system all the time when they were moving huge stones for the pyramids," he said knowingly as if he'd been a bystander. An hour later the white crates were neatly parked by the Farm's main gate.

* * *

Mimi had taken a while to settle into the staid and relaxed life on board a huge passenger liner: nothing remotely resembled her sheltered life at Eagle Court without Alan and Nicholas.

Her breakfast was brought to her cabin each morning by a young Filipino steward; she read in the Library until lunchtime; and she was invariably tucked up in bed with a novel by 9 o'clock.

On this particular morning her breakfast tray had a hand-written message (on a crested P&O card) from the ship's Purser. 'Could you spare a few moments after breakfast to discuss your onward travel arrangements once we reach Perth, as I may be able to assist you with transport or hotel bookings.' It was signed P. Galbraith.

Mimi found smartly-uniformed Mr Galbraith alone in his office at 10.00 am. "To tell you the truth, I haven't really given it a lot of thought – I've been finding the journey so relaxing and the service is superb!"

The Purser gave a nod and a gracious smile to the compliment. "The re-fit hasn't disturbed you?"

Mimi smiled. "If I hadn't been told about it in London, I wouldn't have even known they were there!"

"Well, we're due to dock in Perth at 16.00 hrs tomorrow, but as I'm sure you'll appreciate, these timings can be flexible, what with tides and other shipping." He paused and balanced a pencil on end on his blotter. "On top of which you will have to brace yourself for what could be a long wait in Immigration. These days the Perth authorities are scrupulously thorough." He laid the pencil down. "So where are you headed for first, Mrs Jones?"

"Malvern Creek."

"Which is about a three-hour drive." He opened a bus timetable. "There are two coaches each day from the pick-up point behind the Docks Office, but the afternoon one sets off at 16.30 hrs. You'd be better off staying overnight in a budget hotel portside. There's a Kennedy that's very comfortable – and not expensive. Would you like me to telex them to reserve you a single room?"

"Oh thank you, that would be most kind."

"Is there anything else you need help with?"

"Well, I'd rather hoped to go and see tonight's screening of *Blithe Spirit*."

He smiled as he jotted himself a note. "An excellent choice. It's being screened at 7.00 pm in the small Studio, so I'll reserve you a seat, giving you time to take an early supper in the self-service cafeteria." He smiled and shook his head. "Madame Arcati is wonderful!" Mimi thanked the Purser, left his office, and armed with her book headed for one of the sun lounges, where she intended to read until lunchtime.

"So how are you finding *Jane Eyre*?", a female voice with a distinctive Scottish brogue inquired. Sitting opposite her was a smartly dressed lady in her 50s.

"A bit creepy, actually. I think I should have chosen something lighter." The woman held up an orange-and-white striped Penguin paperback marked *Scoop*. "You can't go wrong with Everlyn Waugh, my dear. I'll lend it to you." After a pause she asked: "And where are you headed, once we reach Perth?"

"A small place called Malvern Creek. I'm going to visit my son who's working on a farm there."

"I'm due to be met by my cousin Derek, who farms at Brockhampton. I think it's about 20 miles on beyond Malvern. But he's not due to pick me up until tomorrow morning. So I've booked a room at The Kennedy for tonight."

"So have I – or at least that nice Purser Mr Galbraith is doing it for me!"

"Splendid. So why don't you travel with us tomorrow? I can easily get Derek to drop you off at your son's farm. I'm Laura, by the way."

"Mimi."

"My… I don't think I've ever met a Mimi before."

"Puccini was my father's favourite composer."

"Ah – *Boheme*, of course."

Mimi glanced at the hand which had shown her *Scoop* and remarked: "Your nails could do with a bit of attention. I used to be a manicurist before I married; would you like me to tidy them up for you?"

Laura graciously accepted Mimi's offer. Five minutes later Mimi returned carrying a long calf wallet, fastened with green ribbon. *"Voila!* My 'torture set'" she announced with a chuckle.

From its silk-lined interior she took out seven onyx-handled tools: long and short nail files; a nail buffer; a dead-skin cuticle 'pusher'; a small phial of Coty skin cream; and matching chromed cuticle and nail scissors.

"Wherever did you find that?"

"In a sale in Fenwicks. Our Bond Street salon was opposite." She twisted its case around to reveal a silver monogrammed 'M P' on its front.

As the experienced manicurist worked away, she reminisced about her days in Bond Street. "We were equidistant from Broadcasting House and Clarridges, which was awfully handy. And the tips from celebrities were always generous. My employer had cultivated a number of famous sportsmen, musicians and broadcasters. Dennis Compton, Roy Plomley, Geraldo. And Hutch was lovely.

"And who was your favourite client?" Laura asked.

Mimi paused momentarily from filing a nail. "Well, Douglas Fairbanks Junior was certainly debonaire and suave; and Charlie Chester's 'off-the-cuff' humour was remarkable. But my all-time favourite was Al Bowlly. And such lovely manners. We always conversed in French." She lifted her file and popped it into its wallet. "I attended his funeral," she added wistfully.

As she moistened Laura's cuticles she added: "The politicians were usually the most boring."

"Why was that, Mimi?"

"If the next chair was empty, they'd flatter and flirt with you. But as soon as another man was seated for a shave or a trim, they'd engage him in conversation in the hope that he'd vote for them." Packing up her implements, she tied the ribbon of her wallet. "Little Mimi didn't exist!"

* * *

Laura wasn't at the screening of *Blithe Spirit* and Mimi next encountered her new friend on deck the following morning as they both watched the final choreographed manoeuvres of two miniscule tugs safely guiding *Lord Nelson* to its docking berth.

Although they sat together in Perth's cavernous Immigration Hall, they were somehow both stunned into silence by the military-like nature of each passenger's cross-examination.

For Mimi, stepping out into the late afternoon sunshine an hour later – and savouring Australian air for the first time – was a huge fillip, which somehow made the prospect of the next 24 hours seem altogether less daunting.

The two travellers breakfasted together in the dining room of The Kennedy, settled their bills and waited in the sunshine for the arrival of Laura's cousin. He arrived in a spotlessly clean black Humber Super Snipe and stowed all their luggage in the saloon's capacious boot.

"Where to first, ladies?" Derek's question had a distinctly Australian twang.

"Mimi says Hollow Tree Farm lies about 20 miles this side of Brockhampton, near Malvern Creek."

"Right you be!"

The Snipe fairly gobbled up the miles, with a silky-smooth ride across large tracts of land 'inhabited' only by small clusters of merino sheep. "Are they all the same variety?" Mimi asked the driver.

"Too right. D'you know how many of 'em there are? I've only got 3000 mind, which is mighty small beer for Australia."

"How many?" Mimi repeated. "Half-a-million?"

In his rear view mirror she saw the driver smirk. "Multiply that by 50 lady!"

'MALVERN CREEK – 6 MILES' was the welcoming message both women spotted from the back seat of the Humber. The empty, unfenced metalled road was now being lightly 'dusted' by wind-borne sand. Still no sign of homesteads or even shanty-like smallholdings, until a gentle descent gave them their first view of Hollow Tree Farm's spread of oddly-mismatched structures: a long agricultural shed, with a little grey tractor parked forlornly outside; seven or eight worst-for-wear single-storey timber cabins; a rather grandiose Assembly Hall; and a long imperious bungalow, fronted by a shaded veranda. On which a military figure wearing a bush hat intensely studied the Humber's arrival through a pair of binoculars.

Derek removed Mimi's cabin trunk from the car's boot, then shook her warmly by the hand. Laura pecked Mimi on the cheek and, sensing that the imminent reunion would probably be an emotional moment, squeezed her tightly and whispered: "Good luck, my dear."

As the Humber Super Snipe quietly purred away, leaving Mimi alone with her trunk, two youthful figures approached her from the direction of the farm school's workshop. One was a tall thin youth of around 19 or 20, wearing khaki shorts and a T-shirt. His diminutive companion, whose hand he held, wore a pleated red tartan skirt and white blouse and was less than half his age. The curious pair came right up to Mimi. The little girl studied her eagerly, checking her clothing carefully without speaking – or letting go of her companion's hand. The boy's expressionless face glanced down at the Cunard luggage label on the top of the cabin trunk, then broke into a broad grin. "Welcome to Hollow Tree Farm, Mrs Mimi Jones!"

* * *

After the emotional reunion at Hollow Tree Farm, Mimi found recuperating in Mrs Salcombe's genteel guest house in Malvern Creek to be positively therapeutic. It had been Betty's suggestion, being at least six miles beyond the clutches of the repulsive Brigadier Perbright, who had not so much as deigned to welcome the English visitor or offer her overnight accommodation.

Mimi found the tiny township rather quaint. She had twice walked to the small Matins Service in the town's Roman Catholic church and had already begun a 'nodding acquaintance' with English ex-pat Father Andrew, who told her how he had emigrated to Australia shortly before the outbreak of war.

On this particularly sunny morning the priest found Mimi sitting in the boarding house's leaf-shaded garden, reading a book. "I hope I'm not disturbing you?" he asked.

"Not in the slightest. Take a seat Andrew and I'll pour you some of Mrs Salcombe's home-made lemon squash."

"Forgive my prying, Mimi, but after this morning's service you seemed rather unsettled."

"I am Andrew; I most certainly am." She closed her book. "I know I've only been here less than three days, but from what I saw of Hollow Tree Farm - and hear odd indiscretions dropped by the children – quite frankly, the less I like it. But I have to thank Our Lord for making me make the journey. Please tell me, Andrew, what should I do for the best? I simply can't desert Nicholas, having come all this way!"

"Right. May I begin at the beginning?"

"Please do."

"My last posting back in England, before I was ordained, was in Spitalfields: you know, 'on the cusp' between the affluent City of London and the impoverished East End? And that was before the Germans started demolishing it! But the most frightening experiences of all were the regular Saturday rallies organised by the odious Oswald Moseley."

"I remember my late husband Alan telling me about them." Mimi re-filled the Padre's glass.

"Vicious, premeditated thuggery, Mimi!"

"But are you suggesting that Brigadier Perbright's farm school is as cruel?"

"Almost. It's an odiously totalitarian regime, he runs there. Did you know that until a year ago he held regular public sessions of corporal punishment? After supper on Saturdays, for boys who had misbehaved? Using the handle of a hockey stick! After an official warning from the Perth authorities it stopped."

"Is he a law unto himself?"

Father Andrew shrugged. "There are guvnors, of course, but they're just 'place men', trotted out for the annual Anzac Day celebrations and given a good feed. And Orpington, Kent (where the farm school charity's headquarters are based) is several thousand miles away. And there's precious little that I can do. I only have a tiny congregation here in Malvern, which I'm desperate to keep. It's obvious that Pirbright is extremely well-connected either in Perth or Canberra or back in the UK."

Mrs Salcombe appeared from the kitchen and asked the Padre if he would like to join them for a cold lunch, but he graciously declined and she left them chatting.

When her landlady was out of earshot, Father Andrew continued his critical peroration. "The fundamental flaw with the system which Perbright administers so rigidly, it seems to me, is that there is no personal nurturing - particularly of the girls (some of whom are only 7 or 8 years old) by the so-called House Mothers. Did you meet any of them?" Mimi shook her head. "Jailers would be a more apt designation. Occasionally one of the younger girls will have an 'accident' during the night: the girl's punishment is to change the bottom sheet, displaying the soiled one outside on the cabin's handrail for all to see!"

"Just over a year ago, two 15-year-old boys from Hollow Tree made a break for it, setting off before dawn to hitch-hike to Melbourne. That's over 600 miles. At nights they slept in parks, scrounged some scraps for breakfast and hitched all day. They got right to the entrance of the Docks and approached a stevedore – hoping they could work their passage back to England."

"What happened to them?"

"Perbright informed the port authorities, who notified the Department of Child Welfare."

"And?"

"He eventually turned up and said he wanted to press charges."

Mimi was close to tears. "Poor little mites."

"They were finally saved from incarceration in a secure Probation Centre and sent back to Malvern."

"And what did the relatives back in England make of all that?"

Andrew gave a sardonic smile and slowly shook his head. "They were doubtless given a 'sanitised' account by Orpington. But to their great credit they still took the matter up with their local MP, who in turn, eventually reported it to the Commonwealth Office."

"And the outcome of the government inquiry?" Mimi wondered.

"Surprise, surprise: no further action needed to be taken as the children had been safely returned to their farm school!"

* * *

After a light salad lunch taken with her landlady, Mimi decided to go shopping. She was still shocked by the Padre's story

"How may I be of assistance, Ma'am?" the prim young sales assistant asked Mimi as she sauntered into the Footwear section of Malvern Creek's well-stocked General Stores.

"Could I see the pale blue sling-backs you've got in the window?"

"Certainly Ma'am." She glanced down at Mimi's feet. "Would it be a 6?"

"Quite correct."

But for a large rotund lady slouched asleep on a chair in the corner of the room, the place was deserted. The girl returned promptly, proffering an opened tissue-lined box containing the pastel blue leather shoes. Mimi lifted one out to inspect it. She was pleasantly surprised to see an Italian maker's name stamped on the heel.

"Mia!" the girl at the counter had swung round to address the comatose figure in the corner.

"Yes ma'am?"

"BOXES!"

"Boxes, ma'am?"

"The empty boxes, Mia. In the back room. Like I told you: you're to squash them all FLAT, then take them out back to the yard and put them on the bottom of the big red skip. RED! Understood?"

"Yes, ma'am." The portly aborigine wearily raised herself from the chair and tottered off.

"I'm so sorry, Madam. These are Italian. Only arrived this week. Please take a seat and you can try them on." If she'd had any disinfectant to hand, she would doubtless have sprayed it over the recently-evacuated chair.

* * *

Terry the taximan (smartly turned out in a blue suit, with a matching blue trilby) arrived promptly at 5.00 pm in his shining blue Ford V8 Pilot, for the special trip to Malvern's cinema. The saloon's tyres even sported fresh white walls. There were to be only three passengers: Lewis, Nick and Betty. The two young men were waiting by the gates of Hollow Tree Farm, but the young cook had yet to emerge from her cabin.

There was a ripple of applause as her roommates sent her on her way. She certainly looked dressed for the part: a gold ribbon in her bobbed blonde hair; a crisp white cotton blouse, her pleated red mini-skirt; knee-length white socks and red patent leather shoes, on loan from Mrs Salcombe. Lewis and Nick both clapped with delight as she took her place between them on the taxi's long back seat. As the Pilot pulled away, the trio spontaneously broke into the first line of their chosen film's hit tune: *"We're off to see The Wizard.........the wonderful Wizard of Oz."*

Malvern Creek's Crystal Rooms had risen to the occasion for this late-afternoon screening. Giant cut-outs of The Lion and the Tin Man flanked the assembly hall's main entrance; and inside the bustling mirrored foyer there was a larger-than-life-sized cut-out of Dorothy, standing beside the entrance to the auditorium, holding its crimson curtain open. And above Dorothy's head hung a silhouette cut-out of the evil green-faced witch, seated on a real bicycle, with a broomstick sticking out of the back basket. "S'truth!" cried Lewis pointing up. "If it isn't Crone 2!"

Mimi (dressed in a pale blue ensemble above her new blue slingbacks) and her landlady were already seated in a corner of the foyer, awaiting the arrival of the trio. "My, don't my daughter's red dancing shoes suit Betty?" Mimi's landlady exclaimed. Betty gave a curtsy. Then she dug into her tiny purse and handed Lewis some money. "Will you get us all ice cream sundaes, please?"

"Sure. I'll be right back."

Betty passed the five seat reservations to Nick for safe keeping and led the way into the Ice Cream Parlour, whose mirrors were also decorated with stills from the movie. They located their sundaes on a corner table marked 'Reserved', but there was no sign of Lewis. By now the overflow bar was getting crowded, with many youngsters – including little Betty – in a state of excitement.

Heads turned towards the doorway marked GENTS CLOAKROOM from which a 'transformed' Lewis emerged: from the cuffs and collar of his felt jacket strands of straw projected, and on his head was a floppy black felt hat with baling twine as a hat band. He was applauded as he bowed and took his seat with other four.

After finishing their drinks, Betty / Dorothy led her party into the auditorium to their reserved seats to more applause. The House lights dimmed, the crimson velvet drapes parted and to the strains of *Somewhere Over the Rainbow* the presentation began.

An hour-and-a-half later the five friends emerged, delighted by the screening. Waving to well-wishers they climbed into the V8 Pilot to be whisked back to Hollow Tree Farm where Betty produced a delicious supper of mushroom omelettes, chips and salad, followed by tinned peaches and ice cream.

* * *

The following morning the intrepid trio had assembled in Hollow Tree Farm's kitchens at first light, with Lewis bringing Mimi in on the pillion of a borrowed BSA Bantam. Betty was busy conjuring up one of her 'fry-ups'.

Cutting 'straight to the Chase' Lewis asked Mimi: "How are your funds holding up?"

Mimi shrugged nervously at the directness of the Kiwi's question. "If you mean 'have I got sufficient dollars right now to buy us two passages back to Blighty' the answer is 'no'. I'm having to pay Mrs Salcombe for my board and lodging, you know?"

"And another snag," Nick interjected, "The Brig's got my passport."

"A minor detail," sniffed Lewis. "I'm sure we can leave that to the light-fingered one."

"Consider it done, bro!" said Betty, bringing to the table a platter almost as big as the one she'd done for the shearers.

"How much would two passages from Perth to Tilbury cost?" Nick asked.

"I'll ask my mate on the travel counter in the Post Office later this morning," Lewis promised as the group tucked into their breakfast.

* * *

Mimi and Lewis sat on a bench outside Malvern's Post Office two hours later. "I'm not travelling steerage, you know!" Mimi said angrily.

"That figure I quoted you is for two to share a twin-berthed cabin, second class on B Deck. My mate says there's still plenty of places. And apart from tips for stewards and bar drinks, that's all you'd need to shell out."

"Even so, Lewis, $420 is an awful lot of money to raise."

"So how much have you got left from what you brought with you?"

"Just over $100. I had to pay for a night at The Kennedy in Perth, which I hadn't budgeted for. But I'm NOT going to cable my brother-in-law in Colombo, if that's going to be your next suggestion," Mimi s snapped irritably. "I got us into this mess; I'm going have to get us out."

"It wasn't, actually. I was going to ask if you've got anything in the way of personal possessions – a watch, jewellery – you'd be willing to pawn?"

"Do they have pawn brokers in Australia?"

"They certainly do. We may be out in the wops here, but on the quiet they do a brisk trade. There's an old fellow up by Father Andrew's – a Mr Mazlin - who might be able to help you out."

"Lewis, I haven't got anything worth $320, dear. Neither has Nick."

"Have you asked him?"

"Well…. no. But I assumed he only came out with some pocket money to spend on the ship."

But Nick's mother's assumption proved well wide of the mark, as she and Lewis were to discover that afternoon, when her son met them in town.

"Your father's gold cigarette case? But you don't even smoke, Nicholas! What on earth possessed you to bring that all the way to Australia?" his mother asked in sheer exasperation.

"Dunno. In case we got burgled at Eagle Court, I suppose. Before Nosey Parker had fitted the mortice lock."

Mimi turned to Lewis. "So, what do we do now?"

"Well, why don't you stroll up to the Presbytery and get Father Andrew to take you to meet his next-door neighbour? You already know what your bottom-line figure is. Like all pawn brokers old Maurice'll haggle." Lewis turned the case over. "I'd say it's easily got to be worth $200."

Mimi followed Father Andrew to the retired pawnbroker's cottage. It could definitely do with a lick of paint she decided. Eventually a stooped old man with a goatee beard, in slippers and a moth-eaten cardigan, opened the cottage door. "Good morning. Father Andrew suggested I should pay you a visit. I have a small gold antique 1930s item – it's from Aspreys of Bond Street in London - that might interest you."

The old man's eyes noticeably brightened at the words 'Aspreys of Bond Street.' "Please to step inside?"

They sat together nervously in Mr Mazlin's front parlour. From her bag Mimi produced a beige chamois leather 'wallet', monogrammed with an 'A'. She placed it on the table before the old pawnbroker.

"I say – what have we got here? This is rather special, isn't it?" He carefully slid the gold cigarette case out. It measured no more than 12 cms x 6 cms and was so paper-thin that there hardly seemed room for a line of cigarettes. The front lid featured a subtly-engraved sun ray pattern.

"I've never been sure what the leather wallet was for," Mimi said nervously.

"Protects the engravings on the front from being scratched by fountain pens in the gent's jacket pocket." He turned it over to inspect the hallmark with an eye glass. "1933. Assayed in London." After a pause he nodded and asked: "Would you be happy with $200 madam?"

"$250 would be even nicer."

"$225?"

Mimi excitedly slapped her hand on the table, like the auctioneer's gavel going down on its pad. "DONE!"

An hour-and-a-half later, seated in the Crystal Room's café, Lewis congratulated Mimi on her 'cruisy lurk'. "When we've finished our milk shakes I'll cut across to the Post Office and reserve that cabin. Nick can bring the passports and dollars in later in the week. If you're happy with that, Mimi?"

Nick's mother grinned, slurped up the last of her drink and gave him a wink. "Chur bro!"

18

ESCAPE

IT WAS JUST after 9 am, three days after the memorable screening of *The Wizard of Oz*. Mimi had been in Australia for just nine days.

Brigadier Perbright waited impatiently for his morning tea, toast and soft-boiled egg to be served to him by Betty at his desk. But there was no sign of the little girl. He called out to his wife Glynis: "What's happened to my breakfast?"

"Betty must have overslept," came the wan reply. Perbright pressed the small brown bakelite button on his desk he used to summon the Farm Manager. He appeared in the Principal's office doorway (as dishevelled as ever) several minutes later. Still no sign of breakfast. "Has the Kiwi shown up?"

"Not yet Brigadier. He probably missed the bus and he's walking in."

"And the Land Rover – did Malvern Motors finish it yesterday?"

"Yes sir. It's going well."

"I should hope so, the amount they charged. *And* they had the brass neck to ask for 50 percent on account. Well, they can jolly well whistle for the balance 'til I'm ready."

"Don't forget we still have to get them to fix the fork lift," the manager reminded him, "we'll be needing it for baling."

"Did the carrier pick up those fleece crates?"

"Yes sir. All safely on their way."

"Right, get Pegasus fuelled up and parked by the main gate. We may need it mid-morning. And when that Kiwi eventually turns up, send him over here."

"Right you be." The Bludger was relieved the inquisition was over so swiftly. A breakfast of Fosters was called for.

The farm school's Principal stepped out onto his veranda to check the weather. A cloudless blue sky indicated another hot day. The sooner they got on the road, the better. As he turned to go back into his office his eye was caught by an irregular pattern in the rounders diamond in front of the children's cabins. Neatly incised in the sand in large letters was the message: 'AUF WIEDERSEHEN COLDITZ' with its cheeky valediction finished with an inverted rounders bat and ball.

Perbright's intuitive antennae were now twitching overtime. He lifted the phone, checked a number in the local directory, and put in a call to Mrs Salcombe's boarding house. Without identifying himself he asked the elderly landlady: "I wonder if I might have a word with your lodger Mrs Mimi Jones?"

"Certainly. I'll bring her to the 'phone."

After a short delay Mrs Salcombe was back on the line. "She's just taking a shower. She says can she ring you back?" The Brigadier concurred, gave his number and rang off.

After more than 10 minutes had elapsed (and still no sign of his breakfast) Mimi had failed to return the Brigadier's call. He rang again. "I'm so sorry; she's had to rush off to church for Matins. She says she'll ring you as soon as she gets back from the service, dearie." Perbright slammed down the phone with irritation and began drumming his fingers on the desk top. No Betty, no breakfast, no Kiwi and snooty Mrs Jones couldn't spare him the time because of the call of the Almighty!

The Brigadier took a canvas fishing bag from the coat stand. Putting into it a copy of the *Malvern Mercury* and a hip flask of brandy he headed for the veranda door, crunching through shards of broken glass on his way out. On this morning, carrying his cane swagger stick, he was wearing his best beige corduroy jodhpurs over polished brown leather puttees and a military jacket.

Passing the cabin signed Kangaroo he noticed through the window that Nick Jones' bed was neatly made, but there was no sign of the big black leather-bound cabin trunk which always sat at the end of the boy's bed.

At the gates of Hollow Tree Farm he found his farm manager standing to attention beside the Land Rover. "Where's it to be, Brigadier?"

"Perth. And as quick as you like." In tense moments like this the Bludger had learned to follow the old army maxim: 'Tis not for us to reason why…'

In the passenger seat Perbright turned to the Shipping News on the back page of the *Mercury.* It told him that Blue Lines' passenger-freighter *SS The Maid of Orleans* was due to leave Perth that afternoon at 16.00 hrs. Though it was already noon, Pegasus should get them to the port in well under 4 hours.

"Damn it, man, won't it go any faster?" the passenger asked irritably.

"I've got my foot flat on the floor, Brigadier. I'm not so sure Malvern Motors made such a good job of fitting the new head gasket, you know." Ominous hissing sounds could be heard emanating from under the bonnet of the 15-year-old ex-Paratroop Regiment Land Rover as it struggled to cope with a gentle gradient on an open road. Pegasus gave a flatulent sigh and its speedometer dropped 5mph. A 12-wheeler rig sailed calmly past them, sounding its air horns.

"My spies are reporting that that English mother who turned up unannounced was seen at a film show in The Crystal Rooms earlier this week. In the company of butter-wouldn't-melt-in-her-mouth Betty and Malvern's nosey Left-Footed cleric."

"Who told you that, Brigadier?"

The Brigadier tapped the side of nis nose. "'Never reveal your sources' as my CO always said." And there the matter lay until Perbright nodded off.

Looming up ahead was a long incline, from which the Brigadier knew there would be a commanding view of Perth and its docks. A huge billboard by the roadside proclaimed:

OPEN CAST MINING. ARCO ARE RECRUITING NOW.

The speedometer showed only 40 mph and the ominous hissing had increased in intensity. Just as they reached the brow the Land Rover's engine cut out. The farm manager just had time to freewheel into a long lay-by, shaded by a stand of redwood trees. He pulled on the hand brake and turned plaintively to his chief for instructions. It was now 12.30 pm.

"Right. As we were starting the climb, did you notice a smallholding on the right, at the bottom?" he snapped, as if quizzing a group of army cadets.

"Can't say I did, Brigadier. I'd got my eyes on the speedo and the water temperature gauge."

"It's got a post box nailed to a telegraph pole, with a cable leading to the farmstead. So, odds are they've got a 'phone. Get back there at the double and ask if you can use it. Ring Malvern Motors and get them to send out their tow truck asap. And tell them it's an emergency."

"Right you be, Brigadier." Glad to be out of the claustrophobic cab, The Bludger grabbed his water bottle and left.

* * *

Perth Docks was surprisingly quiet, with only Mimi and Nick's *Maid of Orleans* being prepared for departure. A young Thai steward wheeled their two cabin trunks away. The four arrivals from Hollow Tree Farm stared blankly at each other.

Betty stepped up to give Nick's hand an extra-tight squeeze. "When will you be back?"

How do you answer a jaw-dropping question like that? From the most adorable ingenue in Western Australia? 'When Perbright's safely behind bars' he would like to have reassured her. "Maybe Betty should come to England? Bring Lewis." The little girl clasped her hands gleefully.

"And we'll all go up to Birmingham to see your Mum," Lewis added "and tell her about that amazing breakfast you cooked for those shearers." Betty clapped.

For the first time, the *Maid of Orleans* roused herself from her slumbers, preparing for departure. Her joyous steam horns echoed across the city.

Nick stepped aside for some final words with his faithful mentor. He nodded back in Betty's direction. "Look after her, mate. There's bound to be recriminations."

"You think so?"

"Vipers like Perbright will always lash out indiscriminately when cornered."

"We'll keep an ultra-low profile for a while and I'll see if I can't get her to train up another girl for some of her kitchen duties."

"Weren't you planning to move on this year and go back home?"

"Yeah, I was. There's a Jackeroo job waiting for me on South Island."

"Then take Betty too."

"What, as a Jackeroo?"

"Why not? She can ride."

Lewis shook his head sagely. "No mate: it's an altogether different league of horsemanship: gymkhana riding and being in the saddle virtually full-time – except when you're sleeping under the stars, rolled up in your blanket."

"But you're a good teacher; Betty's a smart learner – and she adores you like an older brother. Think about it bro."

Lewis rummaged in his pocket, producing a tissue-wrapped object the size of a golf ball. He pressed it into Nick's hand and grasped it tightly with his other hand. "Don't open it until you're at sea, bro. He'll see you both get home safely." Betty stepped forward. Curtsying to Mimi she presented her with a framed copy of the Shearers group photo cut from the *Malvern Mercury*. Then with a final wave she and Lewis turned and set off back to Terry's waiting taxi.

Nick and his mother were pleasantly surprised to be waived through Passport Control, with their Boarding Passes receiving only cursory inspection. It felt like Australia couldn't wait to see the back of them. "Well, I must say," observed Nick, "it's a darned sight easier getting out than coming in!"

* * *

Sweating profusely, Perbright sat forlornly in the crippled Land Rover. He uncorked his hip flask and took another long pull. Snatching up his battered Ghurkha hat and armed with his Zeiss binoculars he made for the crown of the tree plantation. It was cooler at the top, with a head wind coming in from the west, rustling the lofty redwoods. In the foreground was a large stack of felled trees awaiting removal to a saw mill.

The outskirts of Perth were spread out beyond with the distinctive Swan River linking Perth's harbour to the ocean in the shimmering distance. A single twin-stacked passenger liner, its funnels marked by blue and white bands, was the only sizeable vessel berthed.

The crunch of dried foliage signalled a breathless Bludger now standing beside him. "So, what's the news?" rasped the Brigadier without lowering his field glasses. "They're on their way, sir. I reckon they should be here soon after 2.00 pm." But the farm manager's prediction was wildly optimistic as he hadn't taken account of the tow truck driver's mandatory lunch break and it was nearer 3.00 pm when the bright red and gold eight-wheeled Dennis screeched to a halt in the lay-by with its air brakes hissing its arrival.

"G'day mates!" the driver cheerily called down. "What seems to be the trouble?"

The Bludger deferred to his boss to report the suspected failure of the Land Rover's newly-fitted head gasket.

"Right you be. I'll turn her around and we'll soon get you hitched up and back to Malvern."

"No, no you don't understand!" rasped Brigadier Perbright. "We need to go in the *other* direction! Down to Perth Docks. It's urgent, man!"

The driver scratched his head and frowned. "I'm not sure about that Brigadier. Mel said you wanted towing back to Malvern. That's going to take us the best part of three hours without..." The rest of the sentence was drowned out by the plaintiff wailing of the French liner's steam horns. Two long blasts, clearly signalling she was about to set sail.

Through his binoculars Brigadier Perbright focussed on *Maid of Orleans* being gently towed out into the shipping lane, leaving a huge white foam 'carpet' marking her passage seawards. The great Harry Houdini would have approved of this theatrical culmination to such an audacious escape plan.

In utter desperation the Principal of Hollow Tree Farm pulled off his beloved Gurkha hat, threw it onto the ground and stamped on it. The tow truck driver looked on despairingly. "I think we'd better settle old Mussolini down on the bench seat at the back of the cab, don't you, mate? You can have the passenger seat up front with me."

After settling the Principal along the back bench seat the driver swung the tow truck through 180deg and they were off back to Hollow Tree Farm. Perbright barely remained conscious, occasionally groaning. "COLDITZ!" he suddenly called out.

"What's old Benito back there going on about?" the driver asked.

"What was that Brigadier?" the farm manager meekly enquired.

"Ahem… just clearing my throat."

A few miles down the highway the tow truck driver nudged Butcher. "'ow's 'e looking now, mate?"

"Sleeping like a baby."

The driver gave a smirk. "Just wait 'til 'e gets Mel's bill for this Tow-In!"

* * *

The Tow-truck dropped the two men off at the gates of Hollow Tree Farm just after 7.00 pm. Apart from their porch lights all the children's cabins were in darkness. Nor was there any sign of activity in the kitchens. So unless Glynis had thought to organise a salad to be left on a tray in his office, the Brigadier would have to go without his supper. The only thing he found on his desk was a hand-written note from his wife.

'Perth Welfare rang to advise you that the next UK consignment (12 boys and 8 girls) will be arriving from Perth circa 09.00 hrs tomorrow, with a male chaperone who will require overnight accommodation for two nights. Trusting you had a satisfactory trip to Perth. G'

Perbright slumped down, fully clothed, on a chaise lounge near the double doors leading onto the veranda. No food or drink to speak of; an empty hip flask; and no recaptured escapees. "Please… *no more* smart-arsed brats" he offered a prayer to the ceiling. As he rolled onto his side in the forlorn hope of getting 40 winks, the only sound he could hear was broken shards of window glass embedding themselves into his best jacket.

19

HOMEWARDS

NICK AND HIS mother took their time unpacking in their slightly old-fashioned cabin and resolved to take dinner at 7.00 pm. Nick rang for their steward to order two drinks before supper. He was also itching to discover what Lewis's parting gift was. It was bound to be something unusual; something you couldn't guess at, even if you had 10 chances.

He gingerly uncoiled the tissue wrapping to reveal a small hand-carved ivory figure, a mere 4 cms high, of the Buddha. Even at such a tiny scale the carver had faithfully captured the seated figure's distinctive round-shouldered, pensive posture. Nick turned it over in his hands several times before showing it to his mother.

"So what's it to be, Mother? The Grand Dining Room or the standard restaurant?"

"What's the difference?"

"The first one is extra, with a far superior menu but you have to dress up. In Standard Tourist, its lounge suits - all included in our fare."

Mimi flung open her suitcase to search for a formal dress. "Do you think we could afford to celebrate just the once, Nick? As it's our first night at sea and we're homeward bound?"

"I don't see why not."

The *Grand Salon* (to give it its official Blue Line title) was a somewhat austere arrangement, rectangular and occupying two deck levels. As with *Perth Horizon*, there were windows instead of portholes. Here the walls were all in dark mahogany panelling, interspersed with swagged purple velvet drapes. At the for'ard end was a grand green-carpeted entrance staircase, complete with stone bannisters - a design idea copied from Cunard, who before the war had discovered that lady diners enjoyed making grand entrances on their arrival for dinner.

Dominating the whole space was a huge tapestry, hanging above the stage at the end facing the entrance staircase, surmounted by the French national flag and the flag of the city of Orleans. It depicted St Joan in full battle armour, seated on a grey charger caparisoned in crimson. Joan was wearing elbow-length leather gloves, with her left hand holding her helmet on her thigh. The handle of a huge sheathed broad sword (easily taller than her) hung at her left side. Her black hair was cropped short in a 'pageboy' style and at her throat was a white silk cravat.

Nick and his mother stood for a moment on the staircase, taking in the detail. "Rather maudlin for a Dining Room, wouldn't you say?" was Mimi's verdict as memories of the young martyr's tragic end at the hands of the duplicitous English army and churchmen came flooding back.

At a table close by to where they were seated, a swarthy dark-skinned Egyptian gentleman in dinner jacket, accompanied by a large lady wearing a lace shawl and a black mantilla, were sampling their fish course of sole meuniere. The man beckoned their waiter and made stabbing motions at the fish with his knife. "Too many capers! FAR too many!" His partner remained silent, but within moments the Head Waiter was hovering, ringing his hands with regret. The offending fish were removed, while the obsequious Head Waiter returned with a half-bottle of claret – clearly a complimentary gift. The Egyptian nodded as it was uncorked but gave no thanks.

Mimi, who had been studying this little incident, whispered to Nick. "What a thoroughly unpleasant man. He reminds me a little…" she paused to repress a giggle with her napkin… "of Oliver Hardy of Laurel and Hardy. Remember how your father was a huge fan of theirs?" Nick leaned forwards and whispered: "Stuff a cushion up his dj and plonk a small bowler hat on his bald head and he'd be a spitting image." Mimi collapsed in a fit of the giggles just as the poor put-upon Indian waiter arrived with their main course.

As Mimi was gently dabbing her tears away the figure of Major Basset (a fellow passenger who Nick had briefly encountered in the Library) loomed up. "Good evening! Trifle choppy this morning after we left Perth, what?" he barked at Nick.

"Somewhat."

"Are you and your lady wife planning to visit the De Galle Salon later?"

"She's my mother, not my wife. Why, what's on?"

The major coloured a little. "Profuse apologies, dear lady. Well, from 9 until midnight there's Roulette. With a *real* French croupier. Fancy coming along? I'm told Blue Line have made it very authentic."

Mimi answered for both of them, mindful of the perilous state of their 'funds'. "We don't really 'know the ropes', Major."

The Basset Hound wasn't taking 'no' for an answer. "Nothing to it, dear lady. You'll soon pick it up." With which he strolled off, with Mrs Basset on his arm.

As they left the huge dining room, Mimi told the Head Waiter in an audible stage whisper – for the benefit of the sour-faced Egyptian - that their sole meuniere was *"Magnifique."*

They found the De Galle Salon at the aft of the ship, a stair flight up from the grand Dining Room. Play had already commenced. Most couples seated at the long green baize table were in evening clothes. The Major was standing near to the croupier, where he had saved a chair for Mimi. Nick opted to move down the room away from the gaming table, to study a cycling magazine. *"Rein ne va plus"* was an instruction Mimi was to hear many times during the course of the evening.

Major Basset carefully explained the different odds which were paid out on colours, even and odd numbers, columns and single numbers. "And how much do the chips cost?" Mimi whispered, clutching her bag tightly.

"Blacks are £10 sterling; whites are £25." She knew she only had just over £50. She handed the Major her last roll of precious white five pound notes. "I'll be right back, dear lady."

Seated directly across the table was the sullen lady in the mantilla and standing behind her was the swarthy Egyptian. He whispered in her ear and then moved to a far corner of the room, taking a small notebook from his pocket.

The major returned, placing Mimi's five precious black chips in front of her. She watched with fascination as the Spanish

Madonna formed a veritable 'castle' of white chips around the number 17. "What does that signify?" she asked her mentor. "The chips in the middle of the 'castle' will win her 32-1; the others – known as *au coin* - will net 8-1 for each corner. So, 64-1 if 17 comes up."

"And what's he doing?" Mimi nodded towards the Egyptian.

"You're not allowed to make notes at the table. He's memorised a few throws and he's trying to work out when 17 will come up again."

"*Vingt-quatre!*" There was a rattle of chips, mostly being drawn towards the croupier's 'nest'.

"So what's your chosen number?"

"13. Nick's birth date."

"*Rein ne va plus. Seize. Rouge.*"

"Bit too close for comfort," observed the Major obliquely. "Sixteen – which has just come up is directly beneath your number. I'd leave it for two or three throws."

Twenty-eight black was followed by twenty-four, also back. The Egyptian returned from making his calculations, putting his pocket book away. He whispered to his partner who nodded and made no attempt to place any chips.

"How many times can you afford to place a bet?"

Mimi held up one index finger.

"Well, I'd pile in now, if I was you, dear lady. 'Bet the farm' as American poker players say!" Mimi placed her five black chips on 13.

The croupier spun the roulette wheel, then introduced the ivory ball at the onyx bowl's rim, to run counter-clockwise. The revolutions of the two objects seemed interminable. "*Rien ne va plus!*" The slowing ball descended, clattering over several chrome slots before finally settling on 13.

"*Treize noir.*" The lady in the mantilla looked furious.

As the croupier began shuffling lost tokens in Mimi's direction to make up her winning bet, she momentarily rested her head on the Major's shoulder, by way of thanks. And relief. When all her chips were in the couple left the table. The Major followed Mimi to where Nick was sitting in the far corner of the room reading his magazine and proudly set the chips down on the coffee table. "Nick – be an angel and get these cashed into sterling would you, darling?" Their first dinner on board had proved hugely profitable.

* * *

After a light breakfast Nick and his mother decided to venture ashore to explore Gibraltar, where their ship had docked in the early hours of the morning. One of the young Indian stewards was at the bottom of the gang plank helping passengers into taxis. "Please be back by 3.30 pm as we sail promptly at 16.00 hours," he advised them.

I think I'd prefer to walk if you don't mind, darling," Mimi said erecting her parasol. Even at 11.00 am it was already very warm.

"It's much bigger than I imagined," said Nick.

"And doesn't it 'sprawl'? There was me thinking it was a few artisans' cottages clustered around a big rock," was Mimi's verdict. "With only monkeys as neighbours!"

After about 10 minutes they had located the old quarter: quainter, colourful and with winding cobbled alleyways that shut out the glaring sun. Their route led them to a small square, with a fountain in the centre, and several gift shops displaying their wares outside.

"Nick: I really must get a present for Denise. And something for Grandma Belle. Why don't I meet you in that bar over there in three-quarters of an hour?"

The pub Mimi had spotted displayed two patriotic flags (a Union flag and the national orange-and-black Spanish emblem) on either side of a carved wood inn sign proclaiming 'HEARTS OF OAK'. 'Hedging their bets in there' thought Nick. "OK."

Leaving his mother he wandered up an alleyway, past several more gift shops. Then a newsagent and tobacconists. He parted its beaded entranceway. Inside it was beautifully cool. And deserted. The aproned proprietor appeared from a back parlour. "Can I help you?" he enquired in perfect English.

Nick glanced at the vertical stack of sports magazines hanging on the back wall behind the shop counter: bull fighting, swimming, football. In the middle, featuring a dizzying helicopter shot of a long, thin Peloton moving through a pine

111

forest, was what he was looking for: 'AQUI ESTA LA VUELTA!'

"May I see that cycling magazine?" Nick asked. He was disappointed to find that the text was in Spanish, but the action photos more than made up for it. He handed over an English £5 note.

"Would you like your change in pesetas or sterling?" the man enquired.

"I'm not really sure."

"Where are you going next?"

"Down the hill, to meet my mother in the *Hearts of Oak*."

"Then I'd take pesetas, if I was you. They're a bit touchy in there about the English."

Nick pocketed his change, rolled up his cycle magazine and tucked it in his bag. "Thanks for the warning."

The interior of the tavern was something of a revelation, designed to please and appease both the Rock's rival communities. Spanish and Union flags hung behind the bar, from which Sangria wine cocktails and Watneys Red Barrel were both being dispensed. Sporting pictures on the wall behind the bar celebrated Stanley Matthews and Manolete.

Mimi was seated in a quiet corner away from all the noise and bustle. She proudly showed her son her purchases: a box of embroidered handkerchiefs for her sister and a black Spanish fan for her Mother-in-Law. "And what have you got?"

"Only a cycling monthly."

Nick fetched a jug of Sangria from the bar.

They only stayed for half-an-hour in the Anglo-Spanish pub as things were starting to get rather boisterous and headed back to the dockyard. "Impressed?" asked Mimi.

"Not wildly," replied her son.

"Me neither. And we never saw a single ape."

"Oh yes we did: there was a group of them at a corner table in that pub!"

Their poor young steward was still standing at the foot of the gangplank in the sweltering heat when they prepared to re-embark.

"You missed our 'Crossing the Line' ceremony last night, sir."

"Sorry about that but we were both 'bushed' after staying up late playing roulette. Was it good?"

"Yes sir," grinned the youth.

"And let me guess: were you one of the naughty Polliwogs?"

The boy giggled. "Yes, I was!"

Strolling back to their cabin Nick and Mimi had to pass the Purser's Office. In the glass frame announcing the evening's entertainments was a poster depicting the legendary dancing couple of Ginger Rogers and Fred Astaire in a scene from the movie *Flying Down to Rio*.

Mimi grasped her son's arm excitedly and sighed: "Oh do let's have an early supper, Nick – and not in that gloomy mausoleum – so we can see Fred and Ginger? I missed it when it was on at The Majestic – all because your dear father said he had too much paperwork from the War Damage Commission to deal with!"

They opted to take supper in the ship's standard class restaurant at 6.00 pm, to get good seats to see the evening movie in the Ballroom.

"So, what was all that Golliwog stuff?" Mimi enquired over supper.

"Polliwogs are traditional spirits, dating back to Polynesian times, supporters of King Neptune, who appear for the Crossing the Line ceremony when the ship crosses the invisible Equator. They roam around the companionways on the night before creating mischief. Pity you missed it on the way out."

"I'm rather glad I did!"

Nick and Mimi, both famished after not eating in the rowdy Hearts of Oak, happily tucked into the beautifully-presented battered cod and pommes frites that was on offer as the main course in the restaurant, followed by strawberry ice cream.

"Still thinking about your lucky win in the Charles de Gaulle Salon last night?" Nick asked.

"I certainly am. You don't know just how close to the wire we were." To emphasise the point she held up one hand, making the shape of a 'C' with its thumb and forefinger half an inch apart.

"So where did it all go?"

"My taxi to Tilbury. Tips on the ship. The un-budgeted night at The Kennedy Inn in Perth. Mrs Salcombe's board and lodging.

My lovely blue sling backs for the Oz screening – that was the only item of clothing I bought in Australia. A small donation to Father Andrew. Terry the Taximan down to Perth Docks. Oh, and I paid for Betty's red dancing pumps as she adored them so much. So why did you bring your father's cigarette case?"

"I was worried that old Nosey Parker wouldn't get around to fitting that mortice lock on the front door. Daytime break-ins are getting quite common since the end of the war, you know. Right, Mother, ready for *La Carioca*?"

"You bet!"

* * *

Over breakfast the following morning Nick showed his mother the Spanish cycling magazine he had bought in Gibraltar. "There's an English language announcement here at the bottom of the back page which I thought I'd show to Matt when we get back." He slid it across the table.

> **'The British-based newspaper THE BRISTOL POST has announced a 3-day international cycle event, to take place in and around the city of Bristol from 7-10 September 1949. Events will include a time trial, a half-day tour of the countryside and a 2-mile hill climb up to the famous Bristol Suspension Bridge. Entrants must be pre-booked. Details from Box 0908, Bristol BS4 6LA. UK.'**

20

PEA SOUPER

ON THE OUTER reaches of the Thames Estuary they could still have been at sea.

It was dusk and Nick had taken up his favourite look-out position on the fo'c'sle of the returning *Maid of Orleans*. They were about an hour-and-a-half from docking. Mimi was resting after supper.

The French-owned passenger ship was enveloped in a huge cloying fog, which appeared to be mixed with acrid industrial smoke. Visibility was down to less than 50 metres, making the flat Essex and Kent shorelines virtually invisible. And all the while the warning of the ship's fog horn, echoing back off the wharves and factories. Lights from some of the larger industrial developments penetrated the gloom.

It was positively Dickensian. Nick thought of poor Abel Magwitch being transported to the Colonies. In leg irons in the opposite direction. He blessed his mother's brave act of salvation. Those shorn merinos were now light years away, somewhere in the southern hemisphere – while their precious fleeces headed for Blighty. He remembered with affection little Marigold's observation: "Poor things. To think they've been walking around in those thick fur coats for a year!"

The *Maid of Orleans* gave an extra-long blast (as if by recognition) as Tilbury's dockyard buildings hove into sight through the grey gloom. There was hectic activity on the deck below, with small mountains of luggage and cabin trunks being formed by the young Indian stewards.

Suddenly, standing beside him, Nicholas recognised Major Basset, smoking a cigarette fitted with a cigarette holder. His purple velvet smoking jacket could be seen beneath his open gabardine raincoat. "Memsaab's still in the cabin packing, would you believe?" The ship's fog horn sounded again, as if in amusement.

"Mr Jones?" Their young Indian cabin steward was standing at his side. "Your cases and cabin trunk are all loaded, sir. Is someone coming to meet you?"

"No. We've got to take a taxi." He handed the boy a white £5 note.

"Leave it to me, Mr Jones!"

Nick shook the old soldier warmly by the hand and headed below to collect his mother from their cabin. "And thanks for all your guidance at the tables last night!"

Nick and Mimi traipsed behind the agile young steward as he expertly weaved through the lines of disembarking passengers, pulling his trolley. Still the fog's acrid smell lingered in the air, even penetrating the cavernous immigration hall. The Willys Jeeps had all gone.

Through a mixture of smiling, elbowing and sheer determination the young steward secured them a London taxi. Mimi thanked him as he helped her into the back of the cab.

The cockney driver stowed the three heaviest luggage items beside him on the open platform in the front, while Mimi nursed several more parcels and gift packages beside her in the back.

"Where to, guvnor?"

"Wanstead. Hermon Hill."

"Don't know it. Anywhere near The Eagle Hotel?"

"Close."

"'Cor. Talk about a pea souper. 'aven't seen one like this since old Adolf was toppled!"

Hermon Hill and the welcoming gateway of Eagle Court were reached within the hour.

Mimi cautiously stepped across the threshold first. They were delighted to find their home was spotless, with vases filled with cut flowers in every room. Moira's brief note told Mimi that there was a small lasagne pasta dish in the pantry which only needed warming through in the oven. It ended with an enigmatic PS: "Homing pigeons all safely despatched."

On the dining table in the lounge Nick found two neat rows of letters and packages: one – hand-addressed – marked 'BANK OF ENGLAND'. There was also a hand-delivered envelope bearing Uncle Vivian's spidery script (doubtless the latest instalment in the 'Intestate Saga' he thought). Nick's own mail column comprised cycle magazines, a letter marked WALTHAMSTOW TECHNICAL COLLEGE and a progress report from Matt on the restoration of a Victorian alms house at Whipps Cross. Mimi entered with their lasagne served up on two dinner plates.

"D'you think we could celebrate our homecoming with a glass of wine?" Nick asked his mother.

"I don't think we've got any, dear."

"Yes, we have. I know just where to lay my hands on 22 half-bottles of the finest French Sauterne. I'll be right back."

Nick eagerly crossed the gardens to the garage block to check that his trusty green Dayton Flyer hadn't been sold. There it was: gleamingly clean, upright on its stand. He patted its saddle. "I'll take you up to Whipps Cross Hospital tomorrow to have a look at these alms houses," he promised. The only significant change in the garage's contents was that the shelf containing over one hundred back numbers of *The Daily Telegraph* had collapsed. Another 'Clearing up after Alan job', he thought. 'I'll get Sam the Rag & Bone man to take them away.'

Now safely settled back home at Eagle Court, Mimi and Nick resolved to have an early night without even unpacking. Nick placed Mimi's luggage and bags on her newly-made-up bed and dropped off his own belongings in the smaller bedroom. In bed later, his mother decided to take a quick peep at Stephanie's long missive (which had arrived in a fancy blue envelope marked ARCHER FILM PRODUCTIONS). Denise's researches at the Bank of England could wait until the morning.

'My Dear Mimi. As your son's official Chaperone to Australia, I felt I should write to you as soon as I was back on terra firma to tell you of all my experiences, as well as my all-to-brief first impressions of Nicholas's new home: Hollow Tree Farm. I can't tell you how good it is to be back. Two 5-week trans-global crossings, with only a 72-hour break on dry land in between!

'Our outward journey was fine, calling at Gibraltar and Cape Town, including the famous Crossing the Line ceremony at the Equator, with yours truly selected to play the part of the Sea

Goddess Amphitrite! On one very special night Nick and I were honoured to be invited to take dinner at the Captain's Table, would you believe? I think the skipper was extremely impressed by the 'maturity' of your son, Mimi. Incidentally, Nick also struck up a great friendship with an old school chum of your late husband, the WW2 Commando hero Colonel Charles Newman VC, who was travelling with us to attend a Peace Conference in Cape Town.

'Seventy-two hours was hardly sufficient time for me to form a rock-solid impression of Hollow Tree Farm. It is certainly isolated (a 6-mile walk to the nearest township) with no neighbouring farmsteads. All told, there's around 40 of them out there: 10 adults and 30 children, ranging in ages from 7 to 13. I'm afraid it reminded me of a woebegone Warners Holiday Camp I was once taken to visit at Clacton-on-Sea by my parents.

'The uncrowned Queen of Hollow Tree Farm is undoubtedly stoic little 8-year-old Betty, whose father was killed at Dunkerque. Your Nick is the oldest. Activities are divided between morning school classes and afternoon farm work, six days a week. The Principal is a swaggering, militaristic figure known only as The Brigadier, who I didn't like one little bit. His mousy wife Glynis stays largely in the background, although she's supposed to be in charge of the kitchens.

'Right, here's the Good News. I've had to tell Blue Line that I won't be available for any more chaperone sessions to Australia as, awaiting my return, was a letter from Archer Studios, offering me a job as a Continuity Assistant on their next film (I'd sent them my cv and an informal request before I left, but hearing nothing thought no more about it). It's to be called 'A Matter of Life and Death' and we start filming the week-after-next, somewhere on the coast near Bournemouth. I am to be the Personal Assistant of Mr Emeric Pressburger, a Hungarian financier who is co-owner of Archer with the director Michael Powell. It stars – would you believe it – the dishy David Niven, who plays the part of an RAF bomber pilot in the war. I'll be able to fill you in with more details when I see you next. One rather worrying 'challenge' which I've already been given by Mr Pressburger, is to locate the longest escalator in Britain and

negotiate with its owners to let us film on it. I can't for the life of me think what role escalators played in The Battle of Britain!

'I've spoken to Moira a couple of times, but only on the phone. It seems she and Matt have successfully acquired a bijou alms house in the grounds of Whipps Cross Hospital, less than 10 minutes by bike to the department store where she works. Wow! Talk about 'falling on your feet!'

'So how about coming to lunch one Sunday at my flat in Primrose Hill? I'm only a short taxi ride from Camden Town underground station. Bring Moira too. With much love, Stephenie xxx

PS: Still early days yet, but with Messrs Powell and Pressburger the grass never grows under your feet! One Monday morning Emeric had a visit from Miss Deborah Kerr, no less. He is trying to persuade her to take the lead in Archers' next film: Black Narcisus. He won't let me see the script and all he'll tell me is that it's set in a convent in the Himalayas. "So will we be filming in India?" I asked. "Wait and see!" was the only reply I got!'

* * *

Soon after the morning's Nine o'clock News had ended Mimi and her son made plans for their first day back in England. Moira had stocked up the kitchen pantry with enough groceries to get them through the weekend, so Mimi resolved to tackle the mountain of unopened mail, the most significant item being the bulky foolscap manilla envelope marked BANK OF ENGLAND addressed in her sister's handwriting. But she reasoned that because of its likely contents she would put off opening the package until her son went out on his bike.

"I think I'll cycle over to Whipps Cross Hospital. See if I can't locate these alms houses."

"Good idea. Try to be back by one o'clock, dear." Once the front door had closed, she reached for Denise's bulky envelope with trepidation.

'My Dearest Mimi,

I asked at the Post Office about the speed and efficiency of mail via the recently-introduced Aerogramme service to

* * *

Via Eagle Lane and Snaresbrook Road Nick set a good pace, passing the tranquil Eagle Pond and then branching left to cut across the Hollow Ponds, a huge unvegetated gravel quarry always popular with cyclists. In the final months of the war it had briefly been the site of a PoW transit camp.

At the hospital's main gates Nick was given directions to the old alms houses. He cycled slowly past the gaunt Victorian hospital's main block, its open balconies still evidence of where bed-ridden tuberculosis patients would once have been parked outside in the open air. Then down past the long, flat-roofed Modernist-style Herbert Morrison Wing, opened shortly before the start of the war. And there, at the end of a gravelled track, bathed in a pool of sunshine, was a terrace of 5 tiny Victorian cottages, brick-built with steep slated roofs. Judging by the builders' materials and tools neatly stacked outside, it was the left-hand one which was being refurbished – although today there was no sign of any workmen. The other four cottages were padlocked and boarded up.

Peering through the square bay window Nick could see that the front parlour had been freshly replastered. As he shielded the sunlight out with his hand he heard the crunch of car tyres on gravel behind him. Climbing out of a gleaming two-tone Riley Adelphi was the distinctive figure of Mr Bill Worthy, wearing a very natty pair of plus-fours beneath a Fair Isle pullover. "Nicholas my Boy!" boomed the driver. "Welcome home! How very good to see you and in such fine fettle."

Nick smiled at the compliment. "I must say I really like your new car, Uncle Bill."

"You do? The colour scheme was your Aunt Eileen's idea. I wanted all black but she said I'd look like an undertaker! Its cream and black combination reminds me a little of a two-tone pair of leather brogues your father turned up in at our house once. Remember what a natty dresser he was? Eileen looked at them and said: 'Alan – I see you're wearing co-respondent's shoes!' Never saw him in them again." He chuckled at the recollection. "So, when did you get back?"

"Last night. In the middle of all that fog."

"Mother ok?"

Nick smiled at the thought of the relief of their homecoming, etched on her face as they stepped through the flat's front door the previous evening. "Never better. I cycled over to take a crafty peep at Matt and Moira's new abode. I take it, it is theirs now?"

"Yes, all done and dusted by the lawyers I'm pleased to say. Though for some reason the hospital authorities are turning away all other enquiries. I wouldn't be surprised if they don't put them up for auction. You know they're engaged, don't you?"

"No! How wonderful. Wait 'til I tell mother."

"They've gone off to Cromer to celebrate."

"Why Cromer?"

"It seems Moira has a thing about piers – the wooden variety. Right, come and have a quick look around inside," offered his uncle, fishing a bunch of keys from his trouser pocket. "I can't stay long: it's the annual Chigwell v Wanstead Foursomes at

Wanstead Golf Club. I'll try to call in to see your mother after the match. Right, I'll lead the way."

Their 'tour' of the miniscule cottage took less than ten minutes: a short entrance hall, a living room (akin to a Victorian parlour) and scullery was all that was on the ground floor. In a corner of the freshly re-plastered parlour was a small stack of cornices awaiting fixing ('a nice Moira touch' Nick thought to himself). Up a steep flight of stairs was a double bedroom, a boxroom and a tiny bathroom, its fittings laid out awaiting a plumber.

Back outside in the sunshine Bill Worthy confided to Nicholas: "You do realise, young man, that what your mother did in travelling all the way to Australia to rescue you was an act of great bravery?"

"Yes, I certainly do. I shall always be grateful to her."

"…bravery and risk."

"Risk?"

"Indeed. For while you would probably only have been charged with absconding from that dreadful farm school place - had the emigration authorities been alerted of your disappearance and apprehended you - the consequences for your mother would have been far graver."

"They would?"

"Almost certainly. You'd have been sent back to Hollow Tree Farm, but in all probability, Mimi would have been charged with abduction."

"Is that more serious?"

"Ask your lawyer friend Matthew. Removing a minor without permission – especially one whose travelling costs had been jointly financed by the British and Australian governments – would almost certainly have warranted a custodial sentence."

Nick almost dropped the Dayton in disbelief. "Custodial? You mean… prison?"

"More likely a Detention Centre, which in Australia can be even grimmer." Bill Worthy nodded sagely and opened the car door. "Beats me why that Brigadier Perbright didn't just ring the authorities in Perth. But not a word of this when I call round this afternoon. OK?"

"Agreed." Nick glanced at the shining array of instruments set into the Riley's dashboard. "I say, I rather like the dashboard, Uncle Bill."

The burly golfer gave a chuckle. "That was my idea. The standard trim was leather so I asked the dealership whether I could have wood." He ran his fingers lovingly across the surface. "They said 'yes' but it would have to be an extra."

"What is it?"

"Book-matched walnut veneer." He climbed in before adding: "Cost as much as these leather seats."

"S'truth!"

Bill Worthy laughed as he started the Riley's engine. "I see you picked up some 'Strine' when you were down under!"

* * *

Nick meandered slowly back home down Snaresbrook Road, pausing at the bottom of Eagle Lane and dismounting. He was crestfallen to see that poor old Winston was still leaning forwards at 45 degrees on the statue's granite plinth. The bomb site now looked more like a building site, with reclaimed bricks and roofing tiles all neatly stacked in readiness for a re-building operation. But the Prime Minister's distressing appearance had been ignored.

Nick was leaning against the Dayton's cross-bar when the garage's manager Malcom sauntered over.

"Sad sight, isn't it?"

"You can say that again! Why on earth can't they just put a strong rope around him and pull him up straight again!"

"I asked that. Apparently it's solid bronze. Cast by Morris Singers, who do all Henry More's work. They're coming to collect it next week. Hey – would you be interested in having your old job back: on the pumps at night at weekends?"

"Not half! Why what's happened?"

"The bloke I took on to replace you is fine. A Sapper: one of the lucky ones who made it back from Normandy. But the girl – Barbara – is nursing a mother who's been diagnosed with Alzheimer's who sometimes has panic attacks in the night. I've got a feeling she's going to give in her notice."

"Yes please, Malcolm. Just ring me if you need a replacement."

* * *

Back at Eagle Court Nicholas gave his mother a high-speed resume of his visit to Whipps Cross Hospital. "If you ask me, it was pretty darned shrewd of Moira to make a bid for that cottage."

"And getting Bill Worthy to lend them his workforce to carry out the refurbishment. Are you going to ask them if you can lodge there, once you've started at the Tech College?"

"Yes, I will; all in good time. Oh, and by the way – they're engaged!"

"Nicholas! Trust you to forget the most important piece of news! When's the big day?"

"Not fixed yet – probably after Christmas. My personal prediction is that their honeymoon will either be spent at Aberystwyth, Clevedon, Cromer, or Weston-Super-Mare."

"Why those four, dear?"

"Because they've all got piers!"

* * *

After tea Nick disappeared over to his cycle lair, leaving his mother to get supper. He returned just before the 6 o'clock News.

"Guess who I was taking to on the phone this afternoon?"

"The Pope?"

"Nicholas: I've told you before to show more respect for His Holiness. If you must know, it was your old headmaster."

"Old Miller?"

"MISTER Miller!"

"And what did he want? Let me guess: father never paid my last term's fees?"

"If you must know, he rang in response to a letter I sent him before I came out to Australia."

"What about?"

"Well, it was my sister Denise's idea. You remember your suggestion of my advertising French-speaking lessons?"

124

"I do."

"On postcards, in newsagents' windows?"

"That's right."

"Well Denise rejected the plan. Apparently, it's a device used by call girls to advertise their 'services'. Uncle Tommy says all the newsagents in Soho where he works have them."

"Mother – sylvan middle-class Wanstead is hardly seedy Soho, you know?"

"Nevertheless, Denise has vetoed the idea."

"Replacing it with what?"

"Small tutorials, for groups of four or five Forest pupils who are struggling with oral French. No written work. No text books. Just me getting them to practice pronunciation, grammar and things like accents. I suppose I'll have to write on the blackboard in chalk, won't I? Mr Miller is going to talk it through with your French master Mr Barnard, but he's away on a military training course at Colchester this week."

"The Penguin 'square bashing' at an army camp! Now that would be worth seeing!"

"So, what do you think?"

"Fine. I'm sure you'll handle it all efficiently, Mother. I must say I was very impressed with the way you addressed that Maitre d'Hotel on the ship. Has Miller said how much you'll get?"

"Four guineas a week, for a 40-minute class. Next term is 12 weeks. So that's £50. And he says I can use a classroom in the new wing. I think he said it's called The Aston Block."

"That's where my old classroom was!"

"He also hinted that if I could recruit another mother as my companion, so to speak, he'd support the idea of us taking a small accompanied group to somewhere like Paris in the Easter holidays."

21

WESTMINSTER

NICK BARELY STIRRED as his mother placed a mug of tea and a biscuit on his bedside table. She had already had her breakfast when the 8 o'clock pips sounded on the Home Service.

Fully dressed and ready to journey to London, she decided to re-acquaint herself with the mind-numbing barrage of statistics which Denise had carefully assembled after several sessions in the Bank of England's charities records department. Digesting the facts and figures appertaining to a British-based charity's doings the other side of the world was greatly facilitated by copious under-linings in red ink. In the hands of the right advocate the evidence was damning. She slid the papers back into their manilla envelope and placed it beside her 'briefcase' – a carrier bag from Liberty's.

A bleary-eyed Nick appeared in his pyjamas. He glanced at the long line of unopened mail on the dining table, pulling out one marked WALTHAMSTOW TECHNICAL COLLEGE.

"I should open that if I was you. It's probably about that introductory seminar Bill Worthy managed to get you included on. Do you think I should wear a hat?"

Nick slumped down at the table, still half-awake, and spun the envelope around without opening it. "'A hat'? How should I know, Mother. I haven't the foggiest idea where you're going!"

Mimi slid Denise's dossier into her briefcase. "Westminster."

Mimi strode purposefully along the front drive of Eagle Court and down Hermon Hill towards Snaresbrook tube station. It was still only a few minutes after 9.00 am. Small blue-and-white handbills in some ground floor windows notified passers-by that a General Election was in the offing. Nothing triumphant. Just 'VOTE CHURCHILL'.

The Central Line's carriages at Snaresbrook were reasonably uncrowded. Mimi sat, nervously thinking about Denise's dossier, but too scared to bring it out and read it. An easy changeover onto the District Line at Mile End and then five stops before the train drew into Westminster.

At pavement level on Parliament Square the sun was shining brightly. "Can you direct me to the Houses of Parliament?" Mimi asked a young constable. "Certainly Madam. Cross on the pedestrian crossing and follow the iron railings until you see a sign on your left saying VISITORS. Go through that gate which will lead you to a security check. Have you got an appointment?"

"Yes, I have."

"The officer at the desk will check your pass and your belongings."

"Thank you, officer."

As if to hurry Mimi along Big Ben struck 9.45. She had never been this close to the chimes.

The security checks were perfunctory and she was soon seated on a long stone bench in the heart of Westminster Hall where, she was assured by a frock-coated usher, she would be collected at 10.00 am. Neither religious nor secular, its cavernous, echoing volume was nonetheless inspiring. Rough-hewn stone walls rose uninterrupted to a mid-point before a long series of slender undecorated lancet windows cast angled rays of natural light across the stone-flagged floor. At this early hour – it was still 4 hours before a Parliamentary sitting – there were few other members of the public about: just a handful of visitors, like Mimi sitting patiently waiting to be called. Bewigged officials in black gowns scurried in different directions, clutching bulging files. Above it all rose Westminster's most impressive architectural asset: the majestic oak timber roof formed by 13 paired braces, seeming to stretch into infinity.

As the boom of the Great Bell resonated around the 600-year-old hall, a prim white-haired lady carrying a bundle of files approached. "Mrs Mimi Jones?"

Mimi smiled. "That's correct."

"Mr Churchill will see you now. Please step this way."

22

REUNION

FOLLOWING A SHORT golf ball restoration session in Rozel's garage loft, Nick walked down to The George. After rave 'reviews' from Matt and Moira about the French film *La Clé*, he had decided to catch it on its last day's screening. The former Plessey plant was all locked up, with no vehicles or packing cases to be seen in the yard. Even the sign on the railings was gone.

The old Victorian road house was equally deserted, with Manager Raj aimless polishing clean glasses. Deciding it would be politically unwise to comment on the absence of customers, Nick ordered a shandy and settled in his usual corner banquette to read his cycling magazine until the film began.

"Hello stranger. Back from Oz already?" Standing before him, hands in pockets, was Doreen. She was dressed in a stylish double-breasted beige raincoat, with an emerald green silk scarf at her neck.

He smiled and put down the magazine. "No, it just wasn't for me."

"Not cut out for the pioneering lifestyle, eh?" she teased with a grin.

"Bloody primeval, more like. Unheated wooden cabins with rusting tin roofs and no window curtains or mosquito netting, cheese rolls for lunch and a six-mile trek to the nearest township. Forest School, Snaresbrook was like The Ritz in comparison!" He eyed her outfit carefully, having only ever seen her in her white chargehand's coat. "So, tell me all your news."

With her hands still buried in her mac pockets, she shrugged. "They're going to close our operation down. Given us all a fortnight's notice, our wages and P45s - but not a word of thanks."

So tell me, Doreen: what *was* it exactly you used to make in that bunker over the road: paper steamers, reels of glitter, Christmas Tree fairy lights?

She only smiled at the cheeky jibe. "I told you about asking those questions once before, Nick. Don't you remember? If I gave you a straight answer I could finish up in Holloway. So, what brings you in here?"

"I'm going next door to the Kinema to see *La Clé*. Matt and Moira saw it earlier in the week and raved about it."

"What's it about? French, obviously."

"It's a quartet of charming vignettes all about love, according to Moira."

"Mmmm. Not for me then. I'm given it up for Lent! So… going to buy an old flame a drink before you go next door?"

He stood up. "Sure. Your usual Pimms fruit salad?"

"That would be lovely."

When Nick returned from ordering Doreen's drink at the bar, she was seated, with her raincoat unbuttoned, revealing a figure-hugging pink dress. Raj delivered her cocktail.

"Got a job?"

After a long noisy pull on the two straws she replied: "Only part-time. Two evenings a week as a waitress at Dagenham Dogs. In the main restaurant. But I get a free supper after all the punters have left and we divi up the tips. They recently installed a TOTE window in the restaurant's lobby to make betting easier for diners."

"And are any of the other girls working?"

She pulled a face and shook her head. "Nothing worthwhile – oh, except my train driver Gina. She's been accepted by British Railways as a shunter at Stratford Goods Yard; *and* her workmates have elected her as their union official. Management won't know what's hit 'em."

"Still in your garret behind the Odeon?"

"Yup. Of course, I could do with a few more pennies for the housekeeping and utilities, but there's precious little on offer in Ilford at the moment. Unless you fancy nights shelf-stacking in Woolys. Which I don't!" She'd finished her Pimms and looked wistfully into the fruit lining the bottom. "D'you realise it's the big 4 0 for yours truly next year?"

Nick decided to take the plunge as they'd both been avoiding the issue for long enough. "Fancy *La Clé*?"

She slurped up the last of her Pimms and grinned. "Why not!"

"Moira said it was very sexy."

An hour-and-a-half later they left the Kinema, hand-in-hand. "Well, you can tell Moira I agree with her summary."

"Didn't you love that third cameo – the one featuring a gamine Danielle Darrieux, in that semi-transparent negligee? Reminded me of that black and green one of yours!"

"Hell, wasn't that a sexy Sunday?"

"Certainly was."

He paused and looked towards the bus stop. "Look, I'm going to have to make tracks I'm afraid. I'm not on my bike today. Had to run some errands for my Grandmother. I was wondering – how'd you like to meet her? She lives just along The Green from your former place of employment. She can tell you how well we're doing on the nags at the moment."

"I'd love to meet her, Nick" Doreen enthused. "Maybe find out what her system is."

"Seems to be based on horses with funny-sounding names." Nick chuckled. "But it obviously works. We were well in profit in September and October. She never goes out these days; walking to the bottom of the garden is about the furthest she can manage. Why don't I meet you outside the soon-to-be Wanstead Underground Station tomorrow at 12 noon and I'll take you along to Rozel?"

She smiled with relief that their friendship had been renewed. "That would be fine. I'm waitressing tonight, so I'll have the day off. And while we talk nags and dogs you can go and paint golf balls!"

* * *

It was shortly before 12 noon the following day when Nick and Doreen met outside the old Plessey plant. She was wearing the same belted gaberdine raincoat, this time over white leather high heels.

They passed under Rozel's rustic lich gate and up to the double front doors with their Art Nouveau leaded glass. Nick opened the front door with his latch key and gestured Doreen inside.

As they crossed the threshold the giant grandfather clock in the entrance hall struck noon. Doreen stood transfixed; it would have been pointless to converse over its full 'Westminster' chimes. She turned around to admire the period furniture and light fittings. "Blimey: it's like something out of a Philip Marlowe movie."

Through the small Morning Room, Nick led her into his grandmother's spacious kitchen, where she was engrossed in a copy of her 'bible': *Mrs Beaton's Household Management*, opened at an illustrated page entitled: 'Christmas Dishes.' She smiled and nodded as Nick made the introductions. "Grandma: this lady is something of an expert in the field of greyhound racing. And I've told her about our run of good luck on the nags."

"Thanks to young Mr Deveraux! Right Nicholas, now what about my lunchtime 'Nose Paint'? It's gone noon, you know. And fix one for Doreen will you dear?"

"Coming right up, Grandma. Take a seat Doreen, I'll be back presently."

He returned with two small cocktail glasses filled with a rich amber liquid on a silver tray, which he set beside some egg-and-cress sandwiches prepared earlier by Alice. "Italian Vermouth's almost out, Grandma."

"Take a look in the air raid shelter, dear."

After delivering their drinks Nick withdrew gracefully to do a stock take of the restored golf balls in the garage loft.

On his return just under an hour later he found the two women deep in conversation about racing.

"Ever been to Newmarket, dear?" Nick's grandmother asked Doreen, waving her empty glass in the air for a top-up.

"No, I never have Mrs Jones."

"My late husband took me up there on the train from Liverpool Street once. For the New Year meeting. A pretty Suffolk market town with a wonderful race course and exercise downs, which all the stables use every morning. Of course all the tipsters go out there too. My, I've never seen so many pubs in one high street. All inhabited by little people." She chuckled. "Like pigmies they were."

Doreen threw an old-fashioned glance at Nick, as if to question his abilities as a barman. He rolled his eyes.

"Pigmies, Mrs Jones?" Doreen asked with alarm. "In Suffolk?"

"All ex-jockeys and retired stable boys, dear. Seems they can't leave the place. But it was so funny."

Grandma Belle cautiously eased herself out of her kitchen chair and prepared to depart for her afternoon siesta in the Morning Room. "Well, it was lovely meeting you, Doreen. I'm only sorry we can't invite you for Christmas Lunch. But we're 12 at table and I'm superstitious."

"That's perfectly alright, Mrs Jones. We've got a special Christmas Day meeting at Dagenham. I get a free lunch and with any luck the tips should be generous."

"That's the spirit. And mind you keep that grandson of mine in check," was her final advice as she tottered off.

Alone in the kitchen Nick and Doreen held each other closely. "What a lovely old lady," she remarked. "Hey, I hope I'm like that when I get to her age!"

Nick walked Doreen to the front porch as the grandfather clock went through its hourly chiming ritual. She stroked the nape of his neck. "I know she's told me to keep you in check – but how does lunch Chez Moi next Sunday appeal to you?"

"So long as we can have some more ballroom dancing practice."

"Rather!

* * *

Limbering up for his trip to Bristol Nick had decided to transform the garage at Eagle Court (which formerly housed his late father's Rover saloon) into more of a cycle workshop. His mother hadn't mentioned the disappearance of the car since their return from Australia.

Masons had provided several commercial posters to go on the whitewashed brick walls, but pride of place in the centre of the back wall was a *Paris Match* image of the Peleton – in single

132

file - ascending Mont Ventoux. An unwanted work bench from Rozel's garage, freshly scrubbed down and filled with cycling tools and spare parts, sat in the centre of the space.

The garage's side walls also had posters of a 'Gallic flavour', some advertising French wines and beers, others showing stills from famous pre-war French films. Running diagonally across the garage's ceiling line were red and blue Dubonnet pennants.

In a mammoth clear-out of Alan Jones' unwanted detritus, Nick had collected up more than 100 copies of the *Daily Telegraph*, bundling them up with stout string into two heavy bales and setting them down at the roadside's edge for whoever came by first – the council dust lorry or Sam the Rag & Bone man.

It was the latter who was to put in an early-morning appearance on this day.

"Got no use for them old newspapers, then?"

"Not really. Any use to you?"

"Oh, I can get rid of 'em if you gives me an 'and getting 'em up onto the cart."

"Sure." Nick put down his oil can.

"Can't give you nuffink for 'em, mind."

This was the response Nick had anticipated from the old codger. "Pity."

"Got any old magazines you don't want?"

"Such as?"

"*Picture Post. Esquire?*"

"I'll have a look when I go back to the flat."

"Or comics?"

"I've definitely got some *Eagles* in my bedroom. All in good condition."

"Thinking of opening up a bar? The old man asked, confused by all the banners for French drinks.

"No. It just gives me more space to work on my bike."

Together they humped the bundles of the *Daily Telegraph* onto the cart while Dobbin's snout remained firmly in its feed bag.

"So, what'll become of these newspapers?"

"They get shredded at a mill down George Lane, then bagged up for use as roof insulation. Seems the government want us to keep our 'omes warmer. Supposed to save fuel. If I get cold of a night I jist puts me overcoat on."

The discussion about waste paper having reached a conclusion, Nick was about to head back to the kitchen for a morning cup of coffee with his mother. "'course what I could really do wiv," the old scrounger confessed in a semi-whisper "is lead pipe."

Nick had become accustomed to his grandmother's non sequiturs, but this one caught him off guard.

"Lead pipe, you say? Any special reason?"

"'cause it's very vallable jist right now, that's why. Two-inch is favourite." He ground a fist into the palm of his hand with excitement. For a brief moment Nick was tempted to ask if he had a relative who was a groundsman.

Nick scratched his chin. "To be honest It's not something I come across all that often. But I'll certainly bear it in mind."

Sam suddenly got all wistful. "D'you know, if I was able to get me 'ands on, say, enough ten foot lengths of two-inch to fill Dobbin's cart out there… I could retire to the South of France?"

"That valuable?"

He nodded sagely. "That vallable."

Nick momentarily had a vision of Sam, triumphantly riding into Saint Tropez with his wagon loaded with old lead piping.

"You know that block of flats that used to be on the corner opposite the Eagle Garage?"

"I certainly do. Got 'it by a doodle bug, didn't it?"

"That's the one. Fifty flats all smashed to smithereens. Well, I work nights on the pumps at the garage at weekends and there's been a lot of tidying up going on over there lately. They've been tucking all the reuseable stuff like bricks and roofing tiles around the back, in front of the lock-up garages. I wouldn't be surprised if there isn't a stash of lead piping there."

The old man's eyes widened. "You didn't 'appen to notice if it was two-inch, did you?"

"'fraid not. But there was certainly a tidy-old pile of some sort of piping. Could well be the lead you're looking for."

Sam rubbed his hands with glee. "Me and Dobbin will go and pay 'em a visit right away. You never know, they might jist be off 'avin' their tea break. Thanks for the tip." He unfastened the horse's feed bag and with great agility the old man was up on his wooden seat, ready to drive away. "And don't forget them *Eagles*!"

23

BRISTOL

THE PLAN FORMULATED by the trio was to travel to Bristol by train from Paddington, taking the green Dayton with its spares and tools in the Guard's Van. Then a taxi, where Moira had booked them two rooms at The Knighton Guest House in the Clifton Triangle. Before the train left Paddington Nick rang his friend Ted Morris to remind him of the night shifts on the pumps at The Eagle Garage he'd agreed to cover for him.

"I asked about secure storage for your bike and they said we can use a shed in the hotel's back garden," Moira told Nick on the train. "The receptionist says it's lockable, but not really big enough to use as a workshop."

"What do other teams do?" Matt asked.

"Well, in the Tour the big teams always snap up all the best-equipped garages – usually at the Stage starting points," Nick told them. "Bristol's never hosted anything like this before, so I suppose they'll just have to take what's available."

"Let's scout around tomorrow after breakfast. And if it's the Hill Climb on Day 3 you've got your heart set on, I think we should walk the course," Matt advised.

* * *

Armed with a Bristol street map the next day, Matt and Nick paced across Cabot Square. Moira had already set off in search of a Conran kitchen shop.

Nodding at the austere statue of the city's famous 17th century benefactor, Edward Colston, Matthew remarked sourly: "To think that this city's prosperity was all based on slavery – and they still laud it." A black competitor carrying a spare wheel passed them as they were studying the statue.

"Wouldn't you think," Matt asked, poking the granite plinth with his street map, "that with two Brunel masterworks to celebrate in one city, the good burghers of Bristol would scrap this frock-coated old fraud and erect a statue to IKB?"

The passing cyclist tapped Matt on the shoulder. "Well said bruv!"

They crossed over the street to the pedestrian square in front of The Council House, where the young lawyer rummaged in his shoulder bag for the official paperwork he'd brought along. "Stage 3: the hill climb up to the suspension bridge starts here. It says it's a mass start, not at timed intervals, which I presume means every rider for himself from the off."

With little enthusiasm the Wanstead competitor replied: "Yeah, I suppose so."

Their route-finding was aided by the directional signs which had already been fixed to many of the lampposts. After College Green and Queen's Road they passed the university's gaunt Students Union building before climbing the hill up to Victoria Square – its large three-storied villas being the first real signs of the city's affluence. Sections of the roadway here were cobbled.

Beyond the square the road dipped down, to join another steep gradient linking to Clifton Road, where the trio's guest house was located. Then a sharp right and an incline up to a three-way junction by a war memorial, at the eastern end of The Downs, the ultimate architectural showcase of the city's 17th and 18th century opulence. The silhouette of Brunel's masterpiece – decorated with Tour of Bristol buntings - loomed ahead. Matt consulted his watch. "So far, that's taken us just over half-an-hour at a fairly leisurely walking pace. How long on your green Dayton?"

Nick shrugged. "It all depends how crowded it is immediately after the off. If we're all well spaced out I'd say 12-15 minutes. Weather permitting." This was to be a proviso that would turn out to be horribly accurate.

The pair retraced their steps to The Knighton, but there was no sign of Moira. "What say we stroll down to the Clifton Gorge Hotel? Apparently, they've got a large pizzeria in there; we could book a table and go there for supper." Their helpful receptionist had told them to walk to the end Princess Victoria Street.

Prosperous Clifton Village was another Bristol eye-opener. "Imagine a small enclave like this that can support a smart lady's dress shop, two antique dealers, a wine merchant, a very expensive men's hairdressers and more restaurants than you could shake a stick at. Even Chigwell isn't so prosperous. At least, not yet!" was Matt's sardonic take.

Nearing the bottom of the street leading down to the hotel they saw a pair of tall wooden garage doors swung open. A silver Fiat van with Italian plates was parked outside. "I bet that was once a coach house for one of the mansions up on The Downs," Matt observed.

The garage's interior turned out to be a brightly-lit cycle workshop, with spare wheels and tyres hung from the walls. Two wheel-less racing frames stood up-turned on a bench in the centre, with the sprocket wheels of a partially dismantled Campagnolo gear train along the front. The oil cans were all Italian. Various cycle racing posters decorated the side walls – including one of Giro d'Italia's double winner Fausto Coppi - and a huge placard advertising the extreme right-wing Italian newspaper *il Giornale* stretched right across the back wall.

A burly mechanic in racing shorts and an oily T-shirt, with his right forearm decorated with a reverse swastika, strode out from a back room and shouted at Matt and Nick: "FUORI!". They obediently stepped back onto Princess Victoria Street's pavement as he slammed the two huge doors shut. "Charming. Let's go and have a glass of wine in the Clifton Gorge. Preferably not Chianti," suggested the lawyer.

Moira joined them later in the lounge of their small hotel, laden down with packages bearing the Conran logo. "We've booked us an early table at the Avon Gorge's pizzeria," Matt told his fiancée. "I think it might get pretty rowdy later."

* * *

Even at 6.30 in the evening the hotel's large Italian-themed restaurant was crowded and noisy. Matt explained that not all the clientele were cycling enthusiasts: the Avon Gorge boasted the largest casino in Bristol. It wasn't difficult to differentiate between the gamblers and the cyclists.

When their pizzas arrived, Nick told Matt and Moira that he intended to miss Day One of the Tour of Bristol altogether as he wanted to 'walk the route' again to the Speed Hill Climb's summit at the Suspension Bridge.

Moira said she'd be walking across the Downs to visit the Camera Obscura. "Don't look over into the far corner now, but I think we're being watched," she said. Partially shielded by a giant potted palm were the two aggressive Italian mechanics from the morning, still wearing their oily Mussolini T-shirts, reading 'RIP MUSSOLINI 1883-1945'. One had his face buried in a wedge of pizza, while the other just glowered at the English trio. "Friends of yours?" Moira asked, raising an eyebrow.

* * *

In Snaresbrook, Ted Morris arrived promptly at The Eagle Garage at 6.45 pm.

His co-attendant on the pumps, Jack Cooper, was already in the cabin reading the *Evening Standard*. "How d'you do," he said cheerily. After introductions, Manager Malcolm withdrew. "I'm just a relief for tonight and tomorrow," Ted explained, "then you'll be doing weekend nights with my mate Nick Jones. We were at school together." The other man seemed reluctant to converse and so Ted buried himself in his *Melody Maker* to read a review of a recent Ted Heath concert he'd attended.

Ten minutes later there was the roar of a powerful engine, the squeal of brakes, and the distinctive profile of a dark green Lagonda Rapide pulled up outside the attendants' little cabin. Jack dropped his newspaper on the floor. "Aye up. My turn!" he cried excitedly.

With a full tank of fuel, cleaned windscreen and headlamps, the Lagonda roared away as if it had been a pit stop. Jack dropped a half-crown coin into the tips can. "Saw one of them at Brooklands."

"Malcolm tells me you were a Sapper in the last war."

"I certainly was." The response revealed a strong Geordie accent.

"What's the exact definition of 'Sapper'?"

"It's from the French and refers to the time when earth works – trenching and even under-mining of whole castle walls – was the norm. Today, Sappers are the army's heavy lifting division – bridge crossings, mine laying, even road building. We're invariably in the front line." Ted was relieved that his colleague had noticeably brightened up and had become quite forthcoming.

"Malcolm says you were at Normandy."

"Certainly was, Man. And I got back. One of the lucky ones."

"Whereabouts?"

"Omaha Beach. Twenty-four landing craft in the first wave. The Navy calls them Higgins Boats. There really nothing more than glorified plywood punts with outboard motors. Forty of us in each boat, so just under 1000. With all our kit. We'd practised at Sandbanks in Dorset for three solid weeks. We thought it would be a doddle."

"And it wasn't?"

"The sea was calm enough (thankfully because Ike had postponed the invasion by 24 hours) but nobody had warned us about those God-awful 'obelisks' which Jerry had planted right along the coastline at the waters' edge."

"Obelisks?"

"Giant metal structures made out of old railway lines, scaffold poles and tree trunks. Like huge wigwams, they were. All wrapped up with barbed wire. And they'd placed 'em just close enough together to prevent our boats from making a straight run for the shore. To cap it all, the RAF never showed up to give us cover."

"So, what did you do?"

Jack Cooper gave a chuckle. "Well, our pilot was a Cornish fisherman from Mousehole and the cockswain of the local lifeboat. A canny devil who'd obviously had experience of getting in and out of small harbours. He decided to make an angled run into the beach. I must say it was a smart move. He missed two huge obstructions by inches, dropped the Higgins' unloading board and we all jumped onto dry land. Then we lay face down in the sand like we'd been instructed to do, just as Jerry opened up from about 10 machine gun emplacements on an esplanade running along the top of the sand dunes. D'you know

- the spacing between them gun emplacements was identical? Typical bloody Germanic efficiency!

"I lay doggo between two other Sappers. Few of the other landing craft got through, with the result that blokes were jumping into deep water. Lots never even made it to the shoreline." He paused and shook his head, as if reluctant to utter the next sentence. "There were loads of bodies in the water - and I hadn't even got me boots wet!"

From an inside pocket he produced an extremely worn Press cutting folded in four. He opened it and set it down in front of his workmate. It was a grainy image partially out of focus (doubtless caused by the cameraman's shaking hands). The silhouettes of several of the 'obelisks' the Sapper had referred to could be seen in the middle distance. Upturned uniformed bodies were floating in the foreground. After a discreet pause Ted Morris asked: "And how long did all that go on for?"

"It seemed like forever, man – but I guess it was only about 20 minutes. Everyone was flat on the sand. German sharp-shooters were picking off anyone who moved a muscle. Then a big lorry and trailer arrived, the emplacements were all dismantled and the Germans moved off down the coast for some fresh target practice. I kicked the foot of the fellow on my left whose head was turned away from me and called out: 'Are you alright, mate?' but got no response. Did the same to the bloke on my right. Silence. I'd been lying on a French beach between two corpses!

"Then along comes a swaggering Scots RSM in a kilt, white gaiters, belt and gloves, with a huge white plumage on his beret. Talk about a sitting target! He formed four of us into a Detail and told us to dismantle one of the obelisks so's the second wave of Higgins could come into shore."

Headlights shone into the cabin as another customer arrived, briefly relieving the tension of the pump attendant's tragic reminiscence. After serving the driver Ted stepped back inside. "Did Malcolm say what we're to do with petrol coupons?" he asked the Geordie.

"Yes. Cancel 'em with this (he held up a rubber stamp), clip 'em onto the bull dog clip behind the door, then one or other of us sticks 'em in Malcolm's desk in his office at the end of the shift." He took up his narrative again. "So, we set to like good Sappers, dismantling Jerry's scrap-metal wigwam. I crawled back to my knapsack to fetch my reinforced gauntlets as one of the lads pulled the final scaffold pole free. Snag was, its base was mined. The other three in the Detail were blown to pieces." Quietly he folded the Press cutting and put it back in his pocket.

The next customer turned up on a weary and heavily-smoking BSA four-stoke. Jack Cooper stepped outside and greeted the biker, whose 'story' was that he'd got less than half a gallon of fuel in the tank to get him back to Harlow. "Any chance of a small top-up, mate?" he asked cheerily.

"I'd better check with my colleague" Jack cautiously told him as he slipped back into the cabin.

Ted smiled at the ruse. "Get him to show you his fuel gauge."

Moments later the BSA was kicked into action and sped away. "It was half full," said the Geordie with a grin.

"Bloody chancer!"

* * *

After breakfast at The Knighton Moira set off for the Downs. Nick and Matt took the bus down to Cabot Square. The cycling afficionados had all headed out to the start of the first day of the Tour. Perfectionist Nick wanted to walk the hill climb a second time without the distraction of parked cars. His Manager / map-reader announced: "Beyond the Council offices the route swings left up Boyce's Avenue. Then a steep incline passes the Student Assembly building until we hit Victoria Square. Up for it?"

"Lead on!"

Bristol's Victoria Square turned out to be a relatively-traffic-free enclave: handsome three-storey Victorian villas enclosed a leafy two-acre parkland, with the traffic road running around its perimeter. Nick looked down cautiously at the road surface: the tarmac had changed to cobbles. He brushed a cobble with his toe cap, reflecting to no-one in particular: "The surface contact between a cobble stone and a racing tyre can be as little as two centimetres. Add rainwater to that mix and it's lethal."

Sign fixers were wiring the last of the event's yellow-and-black directional arrow-headed signs to lamp standards. Light rain had arrived, giving the square's road surface a dangerously glossed finish; the heavily-cambered third corner looked especially treacherous. "How much further?" the cycle racer asked his Manager.

"A mile at the most."

Marshland's Avenue, a mish-mash of shops and apartment buildings, connected with the wider Clifton Down Road, surfaced in tarmac. Large three-storey mansions – many now smart hotels – led to a roundabout in front of a stone war memorial, facing the listed 19th century terrace of Gloucester Beaufort Buildings. The sign fixers hadn't yet arrived, but it was pretty obvious that the final sprint would be along this section of the B3129, as the distinctive iron profile of Isambard Kingdom Brunel's masterpiece could clearly be seen, framed by a pale blue skyline. The rain had eased off and the road was almost level. Matt glanced down at his folded street map. "Assuming they make you cross the bridge to the far side for the finish, I'd say this last leg – from that war memorial – is less than half a mile. Let's see if we can spot Moira on the Downs."

* * *

Vacating their overnight cabin for the day shift, Ted and Jack sat on a wall in the early morning sunshine. "So where are you headed now?" Ted enquired.

The diffident Geordie gestured towards the Eagle Pond. "Whipps Cross Hospital."

"Visiting someone?"

"No mate; I'm an Outpatient there. Three sessions a week."

Not wishing to pry into what the 'sessions' involved, Ted asked: "Been doing it long?"

"Ever since me Demob." He brightened and began to expand a little. "That's why this night job with Malcolm suits me down to the ground. Whipps is only a short bus ride from my lodgings in Walthamstow and the treatment I'm getting is top rate."

"They've got some good consultant medics up there, I believe."

"Reet canny. Mine's named Astrid. She's Swedish."

"Think you'll keep it up?"

"Don't see why not. The nights and the tips are just about covering my costs and the solicitor I found through the Citizens Advice Bureau is trying to get my pension speeded up."

Talking to a war veteran – one who'd survived Normandy – was frustrating for Ted, who was anxious to offer a helping hand. "I'll walk up past the Eagle Pond with you, if you like. What time is your appointment with Astrid?"

"Not 'til 11.00, man. There's two new ones due to start today - making a total of eight of us."

"All male?"

"One lass. Becky: an ex-auxiliary firefighter from Coventry. Part of one of the crews that tried to save Coventry Cathedral. They suffered 20 fatalities." Ted Morris recalled a Movietone News he'd seen of the Luftwaffe's mammoth incendiary bombing of the city.

"I'd say what she went through was worse than my experience on Omaha Beach. At least I was pretty sure they'd get me back to Blighty. She told us how she saw with her own eyes a great metal beam spanning the cathedral's roof, supported on huge stone corbels, glowing red hot! There was 'showers' of molten lead from the roof's flashings, and burning rafters were falling onto the nave like flaming spears. Horrible."

"So is that what you talk about… in these sessions with Astrid?"

"Mostly. It's known as Post Traumatic Stress Disorder now. Back in World War One they just called it Shell Shock. Sixteen thousand cases on the Somme battlefield alone! Can you imagine that, man?"

Malcolm the garage manager strolled over. "Quiet night?"

Jack Cooper perked up. "Some good tippers – plus a Lagonda Rapide." He thought it would be unwise to mention the scrounger on the BSA motorbike. A lorry marked MORRIS SINGER pulled up in front of the statue of Winston Churchill and Malcolm went over to talk to the driver.

"Shall we make a move?" Ted Morris asked the Geordie.

"Why not?" The Geordie had noticeably perked up. "There's a tea cabin by the hospital gates. I'll buy you one of their jam doughnuts for breakfast if you like?"

* * *

Nick had been up since dawn – half-excited and half-terrified at what he'd let himself in for. He was reminded of the escape from Hollow Tree Farm. Once again, the die was cast. No going back.

The hotel's kitchens were only just coming to life, but he'd managed to scrounge a chocolate croissant and a cup of coffee and was busy in the back garden lubricating the drive chain of his beloved green Dayton Flyer. He was using a small paint brush and his mother's sewing machine oil, when Matt joined him, wearing a dressing gown. "Or-roight me ole mucker?"

"BBC Radio Bristol is forecasting rain over the city by 10," Nick told his manager gloomily. "What time shall we go down to the start?" he asked, giving the wheel rims a final burnishing with wadding.

"Would between 9.30 and 10 be ok for you?"

"Fine."

"Then I'll go and grab some breakfast. Can I bring you anything?"

"A bacon sarni on brown would be good, Bro. And another coffee?"

Matt soon returned with Nick's breakfast, wrapped in a napkin. "They want to know in the kitchens if we'll be in for supper as it's bound to be busy tonight."

"Say 'yes please'. Right, I'm going to get changed now. I'll see you in Reception just before 10."

Matt was waiting for Nick in the entrance hall. Now in full racing trim, above smart pale green shorts he wore a white T-shirt reading: 'DAYTON CYCLES OF LONDON'. Matt patted him on the shoulder and the pair set off from The Knighton, leaving Moira to lie in.

Nick pushed his trusty green Dayton along Clifton Down Road, where all the directional signs were now in place. Overhead, the sky had an ominous grey-black appearance, although the pavements and roads were dry. Traffic diversions from the city centre were obviously in place as they were able to walk in the middle of the road back along Victoria Square, many of whose trees now sported buntings. A carnival atmosphere had arrived.

At 10.30 am, by the approaches to Cabot Square, there were already crowds two and three deep lining the pavement. Nick slipped on his white Bic race cap in the forlorn hope that the crowd might think he was a French 'outcast'. They were passed by a gaggle of scantily-clad girl racers, all on mountain bikes.

In the City square, race officials were inspecting riders' identification badges and explaining that at 11.00 am sharp it would be a mass start, signalled by the waving of a Union flag. The skies had already started to darken.

Four orderly rows of mounted racers – totalling around 100 spotless machines – awaited the official starter's signal. Then they were away: cautiously at first, all sat up in their saddles and looking more like a Sunday afternoon bike ride than a British impression of the Peloton. There was plenty of 'Brizzle Banter' at the back, but no one seemed keen to start any serious racing. 'Are we going to amble like this all the way up to the bridge?' Nick wondered to himself.

But in Clifton Road the pace warmed up. Two breakaway groups – obviously rivals – tried to open up a gap, but they were soon 'reeled in'. Even before he felt the first rain drops, Nick spotted several umbrellas being erected amongst the crowd. He tried desperately to remember where it was that the steeply-cambered cobbled surface began. A sharp left – with the racers bunched up tight – into Victoria Square reminded him. An unsuspecting youngster went down in front of him, but a mass pile-up was averted. Now the rain drops were falling like bullets and pretty quickly Victoria Square had been converted into a skating rink. This seemed to sort the men out from the boys.

He found the relentless greased-steel-on-greased-steel momentum, intensified by the echoing effect of the wet cobbles, almost hypnotic. Nick was now on the extreme left of the second 'lead pack', but suffering the disadvantage of having to cope with a steeper gradient as the cobbles sloped down to a flat stone gulley in front of the pavement's wide granite kerbing.

Suddenly he remembered an electrifying moment he had once witnessed on the Champs Elysee on the final day of the Tour de France, when two Polish domestiques – nose to tail – deliberately rode along the smooth granite rainwater gutter, avoiding the avenue's notorious pavées and gaining a dozen places with their daring manœuvre.

He first slipped the Dayton's front wheel, then the rear wheel, neatly off the cobbles into the rainwater gulley, causing bystanders to take a step back. He had quickly overhauled six riders and was soon surreptitiously tagging onto the back of the 12-strong front pack. But his audacious break-away had attracted attention from behind. He distinctly heard foreign shouts. Then like a thunderbolt from the leaden sky above he felt a violent punch in the small of his back, accompanied by a snarling shout of "FUORI!". The Mussolini brothers sped past on their Italian racing machines.

Releasing his grip momentarily on his bike's handlebars caused Nick's front wheel to first veer right and then to attempt to mount the high granite kerb. Which it failed to do. The three-deep crowd parted like the Red Sea, allowing the green racing cycle to crash into the wall of a large villa, with its dazed rider following immediately behind. Nobody from the crowd stepped forward to offer aid and the only sounds were the raindrops and the relentless 'click-click' of passing derailleur geartrains.

"Please step back! I'm a doctor," were the last words Nick heard before he passed out.

* * *

When he regained consciousness, the bruised and battered cyclist found himself stretched out on an upholstered inspection couch in a brightly-lit private surgery. A white uniformed nurse and a doctor watched him intently as he opened his eyes. The nurse was gently dabbing blood marks from his forehead while the doctor checked his pulse and breathing. "Check for any small lesions on the back of his skull, nurse" the doctor directed.

It quickly emerged that Nick's other injuries were severe lacerations to the left leg, a black eye, a missing tooth and an extremely painful left wrist. The doctor carefully felt around the swelling and told his nurse: "I'll have to make a temporary splint. Look in the top drawer of my desk: there should be a couple of six-inch boxwood rules there."

"Here we are Doctor Mee," the young nurse reported two minutes later. Between them they constructed a make-shift splint, wrapping it up tightly with a cotton bandage. "I'm pretty sure the Royal Infirmary will say it needs a plaster cast," was Nick's saviour's diagnosis. "But it's a brain scan that's the most pressing. I'll ring the hospital from my office. You just keep him calm and settled." Before drifting off again, Nick thought to himself: 'Don't worry, doctor, I'm not planning to go anywhere.'

Since the speed climb's climax up at the Suspension Bridge, Matt and Moira fretted about their friend's non-arrival. No reference to the accident in Victoria Square was made over the PA system. Flower garlands, cups and cheques were distributed and the crowd began to disperse.

Hand-in-hand the couple forlornly retraced their steps in the general direction of their hotel. Rounding the corner of Victoria Square they saw the flashing blue light of an ambulance, parked in front of a private surgery. And there in a crumpled heap by the gate was Nick's Dayton. Although its unconventional green metalflake paint finish bravely twinkled in the light from the street lamps and its Renolds 531 tubing had remained intact, its front wheel now formed a figure-of-eight Barbara Hepworth might have admired. Its Campagnolo 12-speed gear mechanism was neatly spread across the pavement like a row of jagged-edged playing cards.

"Wait here while I see what's going on," Matt told Moira. For all he knew the bike's rider might be a corpse. The surgery's front door was open. Half-way across the hall he met two young paramedics carefully walking Nick towards the waiting ambulance. Nick smiled. "Sorry, mate: I fell at the last fence!"

* * *

Matt and Moira dined alone at the Knighton. Shortly after 10 o'clock Nick was lead in by Dr Mee and his young nurse. All three were smiling. Nick triumphantly held up his left wrist, cast in plaster. "I'll need you all to autograph this before we get the train back to London tomorrow!"

The following morning the remains of the Dayton Flyer were

entrusted to British Road Services, for delivery to Eagle Court. Moira was to leave ahead of them in order to be back at her department store in Leytonstone on the Monday morning.

Nick and Matt took a taxi to Temple Meads Station to catch the mid-morning service to Paddington. They had found an empty compartment when a Pullman Car attendant enquired if they would be taking lunch. "Why not?" Nick asked rhetorically. "Can we have the first sitting?"

"Certainly sir." They followed him to the Restaurant Car.

"And does this service go via the famous Box Tunnel?"

"It most certainly does, sir."

Another Brunel connection, Nick thought. "Are you familiar with the tunnel's history?" he asked, cautiously easing himself into a window seat.

"Up to a point, sir. The history of Box is known to most long-serving GWR employees."

"Then fire away!"

"Well, at the time – the 1840s - it was the longest rail tunnel ever attempted in this country, employing up to 4000 navvies. Brunel did most of the surveying and setting out himself. When the two 'drives' met in the middle beneath Box Hill, there was only a discrepancy of two inches - and after 1.8 miles of hand-excavated tunnelling that's not bad going. Brunel removed his gold signet ring and presented it to the foreman of the tunnellers as a keep-sake."

"And is the legend of the rising sun illuminating the tunnel on Brunel's birthday true?" Nick asked their knowledgeable attendant.

"Only half-true, sir. It shines down the tunnel on 6th April, the great man's sister's birthday! May I get you the wine list?"

"Excellent idea. Thank you."

Seated in a quiet corner of the restaurant car, they settled for French onion soup and rump steaks. Nick studied the wine list and handed it back to the attendant. "Would you be able to rustle up a nice vintage Cotes de Rhone for us?"

"I'm sure I could, sir."

"So have they started making their way across the Channel again?" he asked.

"Not as yet, sir, though I suspect our modest reserve has been buried away in the cellars under St Pancras Station since before the recent hostilities on the continent commenced, sir" he replied. If he wasn't working for GWR, Nick decided, this fellow could walk into a job as Head Butler at any stately home in England.

Matt handed Nick a piece of white cotton, which looked like a spare napkin. "Moira picked this up off the pavement outside that surgery." Nick smiled as he opened it to reveal his Bic cycle hat. Over a pudding of spotted dick and custard the table talk turned to business.

"I don't see how we can up our output any further," Matt began. "Moira's doing everything possible to keep overheads down – free boxes and tissues from Bearmans; she's even negotiated a series discount for our advert with *Exchange & Mart*."

For a man who was still suffering from shock and mild concussion, Nick's response worried his business partner. "Then we'll just have to get ourselves a wet suit – you know, like the frogmen used in the war? Keep it at Rozel, change in the garage before Grandma's up. Clean up with Sunday morning dawn dives before old Banksie arrives."

"Don't be daft. You'd never get away with it," his partner replied dismissively. "At 8 in the morning? Wandering down St Mary's Avenue dressed like The Loch Ness Monster!"

"Actually, I was planning to go on my bike."

"Even dafter! There'd certainly be a black Wolseley with a chrome bell on the front waiting for you by St Mary's Church. You *sure* Dr Mee didn't give you a shot of morphine? No, it's far too risky, Nick - and you know what the consequences would be?"

"What?"

"Prosecution and a certain fine. *And* the end of my career at Bendixsons. Honestly mate – we're doing fine. Minimal overheads, no competition, packaging courtesy Bearmans. Let's hold off from investing in your Loch Ness Monster suit for the moment, shall we?"

Nick decided to put up no further resistance. He stared at his empty pudding plate as the Attendant approached. "Err… what happened to the spotted dick?"

"You ate it, Sir."

24

FLY POSTING

A PURPLE AND BLUE deckled-edged invitation card graced the lounge mantlepiece when Nick arrived home. The invitation intrigued him.

> **A MATTER OF LIFE AND DEATH**
> **Mr Michael Powell & Mr Emeric Pressburger cordially invite you to the London Premier of Archer Films' latest production, to be held at THE ODEON, MARBLE ARCH on Tuesday lst November 1949. Please be in your seats by 6.30 pm. The screening will be followed by a Reception and Buffet Supper at THE CUMBERLAND HOTEL, MARBLE ARCH.**
> **Black tie.**   **RSVP**

Mimi brought her son a reviving cup of hot chocolate after his all-night session at the Eagle Garage. "Busy night?" He very nearly gave her a flippant 'Busier afternoon at Gants Hill' but checked himself just in time. "Not too bad."

Nick's mother nodded proudly at the mantlepiece. "Well, my dear, it's arrived at last. You'll have to hire a dinner jacket from Jennings at Loughton. I've arranged to go and have tea with Eileen Worthy, so I can borrow one of her outfits. Steph rang – just to check that the invitation had arrived and advises us to book a twin-bedded room at the Cumberland Hotel. We can save money that way."

"How come?"

"Go both ways on the Central Line. Provided you don't mind carrying our outfits. I'm dying to know why there's an escalator in it." Nick's mother's non sequiturs now almost outranked Nana Belle's.

"I thought you wanted to meet David Niven."

"Oh yes. That too."

"Fine. I'll get Ted Morris to cover for me at the Eagle Garage again."

"Can't you give it up, dear?"

"The tips are too good, mother. And you know how you've become re-accustomed to Mr Mumford's freshly-milled coffee!"

"Oh and by the way, Mason's rang – Mr Mason himself, no less. Your new bike has arrived!"

* * *

Returning from the first training session on his new bike, Nick found his mother seated in the kitchen studying a hand-written letter. Beside it was an unstamped foolscap blue envelope, its hand-written address in the familiar spindly style of his uncle Vivian. Alongside was the Quality Street exchequer. "I see you've had a communication from The Spider Man. What an honour!"

"That's no way to refer to your uncle, Nicholas. He's doing his best in very difficult circumstances."

Nick could clearly make out a numbered list in the solicitor's distinctive writing on the letter's back page. "Oh yes? So, what's he got to say?"

"Have we found any savings books or War bonds amongst your father's private effects?"

"Nope."

"Do we know anything about some shares in a South African gold mine which your grandfather gave to his three children?"

"First I've ever heard of it."

"Have we received an offer of a new tenancy agreement from Eagle Court's Freeholders?"

"*Niet.*"

"Has the Manager of Wanstead's Westminster Bank notified us yet of an interim overdraft facility?"

"*Jamais.*"

"Have any valuable personal effects, such as a wristwatch or cufflinks come to light?"

"*Non.*"

"Have we received Form WD43 from the War Damage Commission, Finsbury Square yet?

"*Rien.*"

"And finally…" Mimi gave a nervous cough, "Uncle Vivian wants to know what became of your father's ivory-coloured Rover 90 saloon?"

"I'm sorry to say it's caput Mother. As Matt's brother-in-law will confirm, the 90's cylinder head gasket is no longer available as a Rover spare part." He wasn't going to tell her that it was now sharing a well-insulated barn in Epping with a pre-war Morgan three-wheeler and a Morris Oxford shooting break.

Nick leaned back in his chair, pleased to have come through the inquisition unscathed. *"Rien na va plus"* he teased. "Just as well Uncle Vivian didn't ask what became of father's beloved Morning Coat, with the satin lapels. Hand-made in Savile Row by dear old Mr Brickwood. Where yours truly was dutifully despatched, each time there was a wedding, to buy him a white gardenia buttonhole? Even in the depths of winter!"

Mimi lowered the letter. "So, what *did* become of his Morning Coat?"

"I did a rather neat cruisy lurk with the Manager at Jennings yesterday. They've taken it into stock as full payment on the dj they've hired me for Steph's film premiere!"

"You do know the meaning of 'Intestate', I take it?"

"Died without leaving a Will?"

"Well at least your Latin master Mr Lodge taught you something. So, when that undertakers' notice gets published in the *Express & Independent* your late father's creditors will quickly form a queue: Austin Reed, Dickens & Jones, the Eagle Garage, Lobbs of St James, Threshers Wines, Turnbull & Asser, United Dairies… shall I go on?"

"No, I get the picture."

"Well, as Sole Executor your Uncle Vivian would expect to divide up the combined value of Alan's assets – the car, his clothes, jewellery, savings - between them. But from what I can make out, you and Matthew have already 'liquidated' most of these yourselves. And what we haven't spent on just staying alive is in this Quality Street tin. Would that be a fair assessment?"

"Pretty much."

His mother lowered the letter. "Nicholas, I'm not so sure your brief sojourn in Western Australia was such a good idea, you know. Though of course I take full responsibility for organising it – along with your Aunt Denise."

"Why's that, Mother?"

"Lewis and Betty – adorable waifs of the world though they are – have given you a somewhat 'skewed' outlook on life, wouldn't you say?"

"You bet! It's called 'Survival'!"

* * *

Nick sauntered into The George, having just delivered Grandma Belle's huge Christmas turkey, storing it in the basement dry goods store which had served as the family's air raid shelter during the Blitz.

"The butcher says it's all cleaned out, dressed and oven-ready. It weighs 12lbs and I've put it in the old air raid shelter. It should be fine for at least a week. He's covered it with two layers of muslin."

"Thank you dear. So where are you off to now?"

"I thought I'd look in at The George. As it's Friday, Doreen and the Girls are bound to be in there."

And so it proved – though the sparkling repartee of old was now absent, since the receipt of their P45s. Nick found Doreen scrutinising a pile of colourful handbills which Raj had placed on the counter. Featuring the bell of a golden trumpet it announced a New Year's Eve jazz concert in the pub's capacious upstairs ballroom, to be given by one of East London's most famous jazz bands: Freddie Randall's Dixieland Jazz Band ('Edmonton's Finest'). Admission on the door was to be 2/6p. 'You've learned to drive; now come and learn to jive' was its enticing message.

"How about it, girls? Are we up for that?" The chargehand's question was greeted with woops of delight. "Raj here wants to know if you could help him get them stuck up on some notice boards. Any offers?"

"Give me a couple," said Nick. "I'll get one up at my tech college and the other at the Eagle Garage. We get some likely-looking lads in sports cars on the night shifts."

"And I'll take one for the Tote lobby at Dagenham Dogs," Doreen promised.

"Give me one for the Staff Room at Stratford Goods Yard," Gina offered.

Doreen took one further handbill and gave it to Rita. "Be an angel and take this over to Wanstead Squash Courts? D'you know where they are?"

"Not really."

"Behind the Roman Catholic church. You can't miss it; you'll see a big sign in the car park. There's a young Polish refugee works there as a cleaner. Ask her if she'll put it up on their notice board, would you darling?"

"Any more takers?" the chargehand asked. "We'll leave one behind the counter for Matt and Moira to pick up next time they go to the Kinema. How many left, Raj?"

"Three!"

"OK, give me one more," Nick chimed in. I'll post it to Rolo's Records at Leyton. On a Saturday that shop's jazz section is often busier than HMV's in Oxford Street."

"If you put the other two up on your main doors, Raj, it'll all be sorted" said Doreen. "So how about a round of drinks for my girls before we all go back down the salt mines for the last time?"

"Coming up, Missy."

* * *

Returning on foot from The George, Nick delivered a letter at the Wanstead High Street's branch of Westminster Bank. Oblique references by his mother to its contents had led him to believe it was an 11th hour appeal to the bank's manager for a small overdraft – a facility which his Uncle Vivian had so far failed to secure. Funds in the Quality Street Reserve were perilously low. He handed the envelope to a girl cashier.

As he stepped back outside Nick caught the unmistakable aroma of the kitchens of the big British Restaurant next door: it was an unappetising amalgam of over-boiled cabbage, potatoes and coley. BR's reputation was founded on quantity not quality. In Greater London alone there were around 200 such communal eating places, run by the local authorities but funded by the Ministry of Food. For customers the big incentive was that all meals consumed on the premises were deemed to be 'off Ration Book'.

Nick lingered in the lobby. The BBC's morale-boosting *Workers' Playtime* was being piped into the crowded restaurant. Checking that the coast was clear by peering through the entrance door's inspection window, he moved two whist drive and bring-and-buy announcements to make way for The George's colourful jazz handbill, then headed home for a more appetising home-made egg and salad sandwich at Eagle Court.

Nick's tidy cycle workshop was certainly improved by the absence of his father's *Daily Telegraph* collection. He'd made a mental note to start searching for old copies of *Eagles*. After checking tyre pressures and the water level in his BIC-branded flask, he wheeled his new Dayton Elite in the direction of the subway that ran beneath the main line.

He paused at the end of Eagle Lane near the garage. On the opposite corner to the pump attendants' cabin, Old Winnie was missing from his plinth. At the rear of the ruined flats, Dobin was happily grazing on his feed bag, while its delighted owner slid 10' lengths of lead piping into the cart.

As he crossed the main road he spotted a bright red No 20 bus headed for Snaresbrook Station. It flashed its lights twice in recognition and pulled up.

"Hello stranger!" the cheery driver called down from his cab. "Me and Dawn thought you'd bunked off back to Oz!"

"No way! I've started a new three-year course at Walthamstow poly. Got that date for me yet for the re-match?"

"Not yet. They're saying the main road up to Gates Corner is going to be closed 'til after Christmas. Seems Jerry's doodlebug fractured the water main and it's got to be replaced. They've already had complaints about flooded cellars, so Fifty-Five Broadway's put the kibosh on all Shoppers' Day Outs to Epping 'til its fixed. I'll keep you posted."

"Pity, I was looking forward to putting my new bike through its paces." He patted the handlebars of the cream-and-purple

Elite. "No worries, bro. What are you doing on New Year's Eve?"

"Not a lot. I expect we'll have to see in the New Year with Henry Hall on the Light Programme. Like we always do!"

"Then why not break the habit of a lifetime and come to The George, Wanstead? Freddie Randall's giving a New Year's Eve concert. Live - in their big upstairs ballroom!"

The bus driver pulled a long face and shook his head. "Trouble is the missus can't stand jazz bands."

Mounting his new Dayton Nick called back: "Then bring Dawn!"

25

CHRISTMAS AT ROZEL

AT 12 NOON, dressed in a freshly-pressed linen jacket, George (husband of Grandma Belle's housekeeper Alice) opened the front door to the first Christmas visitor: Mr William Worthy, smartly attired in a grey hounds' tooth suit and sporting a Guards tie.

"I say, it's like the Earls Court Motor Show out there," boomed the property specialist stepping inside, nursing a tissue-wrapped magnum of champagne. The commotion he was referring to was a small admiring crowd clustered around his two-tone Riley and the arrival immediately behind it of a sparkling white Jaguar XK120, with Captain Urquhart at the wheel.

After entrusting the champagne to Alice, Bill Worthy went into Rozel's front dining room, to wish a happy Christmas to Grandma Belle, who was flanked by her two sisters Ada and Annie, seated at the huge mahogany dining table, the centrepiece (created by Moira and Poppy) being a glitter-dusted holly wreath entwined with mistletoe. For this Christmas gathering Annie had brought a small copper ear trumpet, but though she would often call out 'What d'he say?' it didn't seem to improve her hearing.

They were shortly joined by Mimi, leading in a dazzlingly-beautiful Stephenie (clutching three presents), dressed in a velvet emerald green and black dress, with a single line of tiny pearls down each sleeve. Behind her stood Captain Tom Urquhart, in his full white naval outfit. Mimi effected all the introductions. Moira, Matt and Nick quickly joined the noisy throng, while Bill Worthy and George withdrew to open the champagne. Stephenie laid her gifts on the dining table in front of Nana Belle, withholding a small package which she handed to Nick. "And this is your Consolation Prize from the Tour of Bristol."

He nervously unfolded the Christmas wrapping to reveal a pair of French chamois leather cycling mittens edged in crimson, on the reverse of which were embossed in gold the initials 'N J'. "Let's hope they bring you better luck next time!"

"Wherever did you find them?" a near-speechless Nick asked. She gave a nonchalant, nothing-to-it shrug. "I bought the gloves at Galerie Lafayette in Paris and someone in the Art Department at Borehamwood kindly did the initials." Probably for someone who had located the country's longest escalator – and persuaded the owners to let it be filmed – tracking down a pair of French cycle mittens was no big deal. With a blush Nick pecked his former chaperone on the cheek just as Poppy and her mother entered, carrying two silver salvers with filled champagne glasses.

Steph's present to Grandma Belle was a huge circular box of Fortnum & Mason's chocolates, while Mimi received her favourite Channel No 5.

"Poppy, dear?" Grandma Belle addressed Alice's daughter. "Be a dear and fetch me that giant Christmas card on the mantlepiece, would you? Then show it to Mr Worthy."

Bill Worthy examined the festive card's internal message. "I say Nana Belle – this is something of a record, isn't it?" he chuckled. "It's the largest Christmas card from a bookmaker to a client that I've ever seen!"

Nana Belle looked delighted at the compliment and nodded at Nick. "Thanks to my partner over there, we were well up in October and November and if we do well on Boxing Day we should be in credit for December as well. Right Poppy, now show that other big card – the one with two people and the horses – to Stephenie, would you dear?"

Poppy brought the second Christmas card to the table and placed it beside Steph's champagne glass. The tall card showed New Zealand's magnificent snow-capped Mount Cook in the background, partially obscured by an orange 'halo' of morning mist. Side-by-side on barren scrubland were two ponies, with a sun-tanned Lewis in jeans and T-shirt, standing holding the harnesses of a black stallion and a smaller chestnut bay with a white baize. Coils of rope hung from his saddle. Seated in a high-backed saddle on the bay was a very grownup-looking Betty. She was wearing tan-coloured leather-fringed riding chaps, a white silk blouse and sported an impressive blonde hair extension which added several inches to her height. The card's simple message read: '*From the Jackeroo Two.*'

Handing it to Tom Steph whispered: "What a Biblical-looking couple! They could be on their way to Nazareth."

Rozel's traditional Christmas spread – this year jointly master-minded by Mimi, Moira, Alice and Poppy – surpassed all expectations, with the two new visitors greatly impressed. After the Loyal Toast Nana Belle insisted on her grandson reading out the text of an Aerogramme which had arrived from her son-in-law in Ceylon.

'As you will doubtless have read in your British newspapers, we are soon to become Sri Lanka. Prime Minister D.S. Senanayake already has his hands full with the stroppy Tamils in the north, who say nothing less than independence will do. Deirdre has her heart set on going to a Swiss finishing school in Lausanne and Diana has been offered a place at a teacher training college in Britain. So, it looks very much as if, in 1950, Wanstead will be seeing an invasion by the Stewart Clan! With Good Wishes to you all at Rozel this Peaceful Yuletide, Bob.'

After the message was greeted with a round of applause, Grandma Belle summoned her grandson to her side. "Pop into the air raid shelter and see if there's a couple more bottles of champagne. If there is, get George to open them would you dear?"

As glasses were being replenished, the Mistress of Rozel tapped the side of hers with a spoon.

"As you will probably know Moira and Nick's best friend Matt have been seeing each other ever since they met at Alan's funeral. And yesterday, they came to see me to tell me that they would be 'tying the knot' sometime in the Spring. They've asked me if I would honour them by permitting their wedding reception to be held here at Rozel; a request which I readily agreed to. So let us drink a toast to the happy couple, shall we?"

Excuses for toasts at Rozel seemed plentiful this year. Mid-afternoon, Poppy came up to Nick and whispered "There's a lady on the 'phone for you."

It was a very excited Doreen ringing to wish him Happy Christmas. "And tell your Gran I've just had a two-dog double come up. Netted me 120 quid! When can we celebrate?"

"Well, it'll soon be New Year's Eve. Remember: Jazz at The George?"

"Don't worry, sweetie: it's pencilled in. Me and four of the girls will be coming up from Gants Hill by taxi. And I've told 'em there might be an extra passenger going home!

* * *

Mid-afternoon. After tea had been taken Mimi slowly began the task of clearing away the tea things with Poppy, while Steph and Alice got ready in the scullery to wash and dry.

Nick followed Tom Urquhart into Rozel's long Drawing Room, in the hope of gleaning a few words of wisdom about Lewis' surprise move to South Island. Alice had lit a glorious log fire in the room's huge fireplace: a High Victorian number in pink marble, surmounted by a brass eagle.

After briefly warming himself before the flames Urquart stepped across the room to inspect the contents of a tall glazed ebony display cabinet, containing myriad family mementos. Propped up behind a silver filagree gondola was a small photograph of Nick's twin cousins dressed in their white Confirmation dresses, holding the hands of a Ceylonese Bishop. It was flanked by postcards of the famous Kandy *Perahera* procession and Adam's Peak at dawn. As he straightened himself up the skipper spotted a large black object reflected in one of the cabinet's doors. He turned around.

"I say: what have we got here? A Beckstein grand, no less! Full size?"

"Only three-quarters," Nick responded apologetically.

Tom Urquart cautiously lifted the keyboard's polished black lid. "May I?"

"Of course."

The visitor pulled a heavy black piano stool out. "Does anyone in the house play it?"

"Sadly 'no'. But Alice polishes it assiduously every week!"

Tom moved round to settle himself at the keyboard. "Then I suspect it may need tuning." He softly played a chord and then a second, with and without the reverberation peddle, nodded and lent back on the stool. "A thought has just occurred to me, Nicholas."

"And that is?"

"When the date of your friends' wedding reception is known, telegraph it at once to Steph. And if it doesn't fall within the middle of one of my trips to Perth, I dare say I could persuade Miss Fernside to come to play here in the afternoon. What do you think?"

"I think it's an absolutely brilliant idea! But would she accept?"

"Like a shot. She's told me she's not keen on big formal recitals - though personally I thought she handled your Billie Holiday medley with great aplomb." He glanced around the room, as if measuring its capacity. "She much prefers small intimate family gatherings, as I imagine Moira and Matt's will be. She was a professional music teacher; taught at one of the Oxford colleges." He nodded in the direction of the conservatory. "And with those French windows open, the guests will be able to stand in the garden."

Stephanie wandered in carrying a tea towel. "Plotting?"

Both men giggled. "Sort of," replied Nick.

Tom Urquhart placed his hands back on the keyboard and then wholly without prompting played the first two lines of the popular Al Bowlly classic *"Love is the sweetest thing."*

Moments later Mimi was standing in the Drawing Room's doorway, clutching a tea towel and looking none too pleased. "Nicholas?"

"Yes Mother?"

"I sincerely trust you have not opened negotiations with Captain Urquhart to sell him Grandma's Beckstein grand?"

The skipper rocked on the stool with laughter. "Perish the thought, dear lady. We were considering the idea of a live musical accompaniment for Moira and Matt's forthcoming nuptials." After executing a very professional *glissando* he cautiously began the second coda. And as the nostalgic Bowlly melody flooded out of the Beckstein filling the Drawing Room, Mimi excused herself, saying she needed to fetch a hankie. Tom gave Nick a wink and Stephenie gave him a hug.

Alice, Poppy and Moira were clearing and washing up, as Matt prepared to accompany Nana Belle's two sisters home to Forest Gate by taxi. As he waited in the Hall for Aunt Annie to appear from the Dining Room, Nana Belle called from the kitchen: "Matthew – don't forget Annie's trumpet!" For a nano-second the young solicitor (unfamiliar with the matriarch's legendary non sequiturs) envisaged Annie, shoulder-to-shoulder with Freddie Randall, blowing a duet on the Satchmo classic *When Its Sleepy Time Down South* in The George's great ballroom. He opened his eyes to find Poppy offering him a coiled copper tube. "Miss Farmer's hearing aid," the child prompted.

26

FINIS

NICK'S SAFE RETURN to Blighty, followed immediately by the Bristol cycling event and accident, had somewhat put arrangements for his attendance at Walthamstow Technical College into the shade. To further add complications, he was very nearly late for the introductory lecture by the Head of the Structural Engineering Department, Mr Navotni.

Having safely stored his new white-and-purple Dayton Elite, Nick made a dash for the central Lecture Hall and entered just as the lights were being dimmed. Navotni's unassuming manner was in stark contrast to Forest School's be-gowned thespians. The opportunity of getting to grips with the finer points of structural engineering made the next forty-five minutes all the more enticing.

"I've taken just four projects of international significance to look at with you today. You are probably familiar with most of them, though I doubt there are many students here who have stood on the viewing gallery of the Empire State Building. My 'thesis', if you will, is that in most large-scale construction projects – the Empire State Building being a classic case – the pioneering problem-solving work of the structural engineer is all too often overshadowed by the 'design pyrotechnics' of the project's team of architects. It was ever thus. Right back to the Colosseum."

The hall was then filled with a gold-and-scarlet slide image of one of the Empire State Building's public viewing galleries, its huge opened bronze double doors decorated with abstract Art Deco designs. "It was designed by Shreve and Harmon, with the structural engineering input coming from Home Gage Balcom. The core of this monumental structure is a riveted steel frame of 365,000 tons. Can you believe that this magnificent 443m-high monolith was completed in only 13 months and is still the world's tallest tower?" The French modernist pioneer Le Corbusier – never backward and coming forward with his opinions – travelled to New York on the French luxury liner *Normandie* expressly to see the mighty Empire State Building at first hand. In his diary he described Manhattan as a dream city: 'a vision of enchantment'. But up close he had deep reservations that 'this monolithic world might trample the living city under its huge feet'. "Not bad for a fleeting glimpse by a foreigner."

The Hungarian lecturer then clicked rapidly through a half-dozen more images, before abruptly stopping at a panoramic view of The Great Egyptian Pyramid of Giza. "Now, ladies and gentlemen, we have stepped back in time by 4 millennia. For the rivetted man-made steel of Manhattan the Egyptians had only limestone with which to craft this huge structure – though their ingenuity, in terms of the Pyramid's internal configuration - was as advanced as Home Gage Balcom's in Manhattan."

After Giza, the speaker showed an aerial view of Stonehenge at dusk, with the distinctive portal-like shadows of the stones projected across green turf. "Now we're on home soil," Navotni enthused. "I'm sure there are many of you who have marvelled at the wonders of Stonehenge, both of its original purpose and its construction. Once again, there were no engineers on hand to devise constructional solutions, though such ageless devices as column-and-beam served them well."

"Finally, no high-speed dash through engineering history would be complete without the inclusion of Isambard Kingdon Brunel. His *SS Great Britain* trans-Atlantic steamer; his tunnel beneath Box Hill in Surrey; Paddington Station; the iconic Clifton Suspension Bridge. Some of you in the audience may cavil at my choice of the Great Man's ingenious rail crossing of the River Tamar in Cornwall. A slide appeared on the screen of a train crossing a river. This is his Royal Albert Bridge, opened in 1859. It is like Clifton – but 21 metres longer – and features double-elliptical Lenticular Trusses, an ingenious geometric device which Brunel 'borrowed' from Stephenson's rail bridge across the River Tyne. I like to think it's possible that the two great engineers discussed the Tamar crossing's challenge together.

"Tamar relies for its support from a central iron column set mid-way across the water, anchored to the river bed 340 m below. It was a huge success when it opened as Cornish people (then reliant on a small ferry) wanted an easy way to travel to Plymouth. Sadly, the great man couldn't attend the Royal opening and died later that same year, at the age of 53."

The lecturer checked his watch. "I seem to have finished a few minutes early. Thank you very much for your attention; I shan't detain you. Next week we will be back in the 19th and 20th centuries, celebrating the heroic talents of three more multi-talented engineers: Williman Henry Barlow – a name with which you may not be familiar, but whose achievements included the design of a tie-less train rail, as well as the completion of the Clifton Suspension Bridge after Brunel's death; the Frenchman Gustave Eiffel; and the creator of the majestic – but ill-fated - Crystal Palace, Joseph Paxton. If time permits, I'd also like to introduce you to the magnificent iron-and-glass roof atop Madrid's Atocha Station in which Eiffel had a hand, pre-dating his Paris tower by 36 years."

A final slide appeared on the screen, causing laughter all around the hall. It was the iconic movie still of King Kong, atop the Empire States Building, clutching Fay Wray. "Pray continue your studies of the Empire State Building – with or without Kong and the Scream Queen! Good morning."

Nick was quite taken aback by the lecturer's modesty and sense of humour. 'Imagine Barnard or Buncher finishing before the bell rang?' he thought. 'The Penguin would have had us all marching on the spot; the Head of Music would probably have had got us to do the last verse of *For All the Saints*, with all the organ stops pulled out!' Pulling on his new French racing mittens he headed for the cycle sheds to collect the Dayton.

* * *

Mimi's late rising on this same morning had been to listen to Roy Plomley's *Desert Island Disks* on the BBC's Light Programme. It was exactly eight months to the day since she had travelled to Westminster to meet Mr Churchill. She was well aware of the embossed blue envelope, marked HOUSE OF COMMONS, set on the mantlepiece between Lewis's picture card from South Island and the invitation to *A Matter of Life and Death*. Still in her nightdress, she took it back into her bedroom and sat at her dressing table. Taking her manicure wallet from the middle drawer she removed her favourite nail file. Nothing but the best for Britain's wartime leader. It was dated: 3rd January 1950.

**FROM THE OFFICE OF
SIR WINSTON CHURCHILL, OM CH MP**

Dear Mrs Jones,

Further to your initial meeting with Sir Winston shortly before the General Election, he has asked me write to you to appraise you of the current situation vis-à-vis your concerns about aspects the running of the Anglo-Australian farm school system for British war orphans.

The respective Secretariats in Whitehall and Canberra have now agreed that a 4-person Study Group should be set up, comprising education and child welfare experts. They will inspect the farm schools' residential, teaching and catering facilities; and will endeavour to interview Principals and staff.

The Study Group's report will be sent to the commissioning departments in Whitehall and Canberra with recommendations (where appropriate) for any remedial action.

Please do not discuss the contents of this letter with anyone except your son. Sir Winston asks me to tell you that he is extremely pleased with the progress thus far.

Yours sincerely
Eleanor Griffiths